BACKYARD RESCUE

Afterward, we fed Rocky and Nutkin. The three of our charges had outdoor pens now, thanks to Greta's dad. This made cleaning them much easier. All we had to do was shut the animals up in their sleeping compartments and then go inside their pens with rakes. Now, while we were scraping up droppings, Greta's dad appeared at the back door.

"Girls, come on in," he said. "I need to talk to you."

My first thought was that he had been hired someplace five hundred miles away. But he looked too upset for that. He would have looked happy if he had just landed a job. Maybe somebody died.

"I just got a call from the state Department of Fish and Game," he began after we had sat down.

At these words, Greta's face went white, and my own began to burn, so I knew it was turning red. We waited for him to say more, but he took his time.

Printed in the United States of America.
The text type is Bitstream Classical Garamond.

The Library of Congress has cataloged the Tambourine Books
edition of *Backyard Rescue* as follows:
Ryden, Hope. Backyard rescue/by Hope Ryden; illustrated by
Ted Rand.—1st ed. p. cm.
Summary: Ten-year-olds Greta and Lindsay are best friends
who share an interest in rescuing and rehabilitating wildlife.
But when Greta's unemployed father gets a job in another
town, Lindsay is afraid she'll lose Greta's friendship.
ISBN 0-688-12880-7 (TR)
[1. Friendship—Fiction. 2. Wildlife rescue—Fiction.
3. Animals—Fiction.] I. Rand, Ted, ill. II. Title.
PZ7.R95895Ba 1994 [Fic]—dc20 93-11683 CIP AC

10 9 8 7 6 5 4 3 2
First Beech Tree Edition, 1997
ISBN 0-688-15496-4

HOPE RYDEN

BACKYARD RESCUE

pictures by TED RAND

A Beech Tree Paperback Book
New York

CHAPTER
ONE

Greta Mallard and I have been best friends ever since we were six years old. It started over caterpillars. Even though we live only two blocks apart, we go to different schools, so I wouldn't have gotten to know Greta if she hadn't been covered with caterpillars, just when I happened to be passing her house.

"Yuck. Why are you letting all those things crawl up your arms?" I had to ask.

"I'm saving them from my grandmother," she replied.

I didn't understand what she was doing, but I liked the idea of a kid taking charge like that.

"What does your grandmother do to caterpillars? I mean, why do you have to save them *from* her?"

"She kills them every way she can. She stomps on them, sprays them with poison, drowns them with the hose."

"It's gross to step on a caterpillar," I said, still not understanding what it was all about. "Their insides are yellow goo. Does she really step on them?"

"On purpose."

As we talked, Greta plucked caterpillars from her shirt and popped them into a glass jar.

"What are you going to do with them?" I asked.

"Put them in my sandbox with the others," she replied.

I followed her into her backyard, which was mostly a vegetable garden.

"This is the reason my grandmother hates caterpillars." Greta waved an arm at the garden. "She says they eat her tomatoes. She's turned this yard into a farm. I used to have a swing back here. Now all there's room for is this old sandbox, which I don't even use anymore."

I began to sympathize with Greta. Even more so after she told me how her grandmother had come to live with her family in the spring. That meant she had to give up half her bedroom.

"I wouldn't mind, except she gives me orders all the time," Greta went on. "And she kills everything that moves."

"Maybe I could help you save caterpillars from your grandmother," I volunteered.

I could see the sandbox was alive with them, not just dozens, but hundreds. Greta had been collecting them from every yard on the block all morning. The idea, she said, was that she could watch and protect them better if they were all in one place. Otherwise they could crawl where her grandmother might see them.

All this seems silly now, but you have to understand that we were only six years old at the time. I pitched right in and helped search the block for caterpillars to save. Greta gave me her jar, so I wouldn't have to have them crawling all over my sweatshirt. At that age I was still sort of squeamish. Little did I know what Greta and I would be doing four years later.

We didn't talk much as we worked. I told her my name was Lindsay and she told me hers. If she had lived on the opposite side of her street, we would have been in the same first-grade class at Logan School, but her street was a dividing line. All the kids who lived on her side went to Horace Mann.

Going to different schools didn't stop us from becoming best friends, though. From the first day we met, we could tell we liked each other. She's the type who knows exactly what she wants and goes for it. I like that a lot. I never know exactly what I want to do. Everything attracts me, and sometimes I just do nothing, because even that interests me. I like to dream, I guess. And Greta looks like I wish I looked. She has thick brown curly hair, and she wears it all different ways. Mine is straight and blond and so silky it won't even hold a braid.

Our families are different too. Her father used to work at a factory until he was laid off last year. Greta says he has tried to get a job every day since, but has had no luck. Her mother works in her school's office. I sure wouldn't want my mom to go to my school with me and talk to my teacher every day.

My mom doesn't work. She says three kids are enough of a career for her. I'm the youngest, so maybe by the time I'm in high school she'll take something up. Anyway, she doesn't have to work because my dad says he makes enough money to support us. He's a lawyer.

Greta's family never goes anyplace. Mine is always planning excursions and trips. My father says he is giving us "advantages." He likes to explain things. At meals he does most of the talking. Greta's father hardly ever speaks. When I have a meal with them, we girls do most of the talking. Greta's mother seems to like hearing what we have to say. At least she smiles and laughs with us.

When Greta comes to our house to eat, she doesn't understand that she isn't supposed to talk so much, and I think she makes my father a little mad. He wouldn't show it, though. My mother seems quite amazed by her. Once after Greta had talked throughout dinner, my mother remarked privately to me, "She has so much confidence. I wonder where that comes from."

That's what I like about her. She makes herself at home anywhere, and she doesn't worry about what people think of her. I wish I could be like that.

Both of us have brothers who are nothing but trouble. Hers is younger and a brat. My two brothers are older, and they tease me until I go crazy. I don't know why boys have to act so bad.

That first day Greta and I met was unforgettable. We collected every kind of caterpillar there is, I think. Some were striped, some were banded. Some were fuzzy, some were smooth. Some were fat, some were long. After a while, I got used to handling them and didn't feel all creepy when they crawled on my arms.

It's hard to believe that a caterpillar turns into a butterfly. They don't have anything at all in common. But I guess it's just as strange that a kid turns into an adult. I never want to be like a grown-up. They don't have much fun. Greta and I are planning to live next door to each other when we grow up, and raise horses and dogs and keep a few cats. I guess we'll have to marry men who like animals.

Greta pointed out that we weren't just saving caterpillars from her grandmother. We were actually saving butterflies. That made the job seem even more important.

All that morning we went into backyards and gardens where we had no business being. Since I didn't know any of the people on her block, I was afraid some of them might be crabby and might even chase us. But Greta wasn't afraid of anything at all. She was only interested in one thing: saving caterpillars.

"Oh, look, you found a woolly bear." She suddenly became interested in a gold-and-black fuzzy crawler in my jar.

"Do all of these caterpillars have names?" I asked.

"I suppose so. I only know the name of that one. But we could name the others ourselves."

That was fun.

"This fat one is the Jolly Green Giant," I announced.

"This itsy-bitsy one is Tiny Tim," she said.

"Here's Hairy."

"This ugly one is Albert. That's my brother's name."

We didn't just collect those caterpillars once. After dumping each load in the sandbox, we noticed that many of the ones we had brought back earlier had made their escape and were inching their way across the Mallards' backyard, heading for Greta's grandmother's vegetable garden.

We scrambled after them, but it seemed a lost cause. By the time we got those strays back into the sandbox, more had escaped. Greta went inside to her basement and came back with a big canvas spattered with dried paint. We covered the top of the sandbox with this—and just in time. For at that moment her grandmother called out the window that it was time to come in for lunch.

I had forgotten about lunch, myself. Now I ran

home, hoping that my mother wasn't worrying about me. I hadn't told her where I was going or how long I would be gone because I didn't know that I was going to meet someone like Greta and get involved in a caterpillar project. This time I was in luck. My mom was setting up card tables for her bridge club and hadn't even noticed I was gone.

"Wash your hands, dear. How did they get so dirty? Marie has lunch for you in the kitchen," she said.

I was off the hook.

I didn't see Greta for two days after that. Then I went over to her house and rang the front doorbell. She seemed really glad to see me.

"Come on in," she said. "I'm grounded."

"You can't come out?" I asked in amazement. This had never happened to me. "What did you do?"

"It was the caterpillars," she said. "Come, let me show you."

She led me to the dining room window, which looked out on what had once been a vegetable garden.

"They dee-stroyed it." She made a dramatic sweeping motion with her arm to emphasize the extent of the damage.

"Your grandmother's garden is gone?"

"Totaled," she said with a hint of satisfaction.

That it was. I stared at the devastation. Every leaf had either been entirely eaten or was hanging lacy and dead on brown stalks. What a scene there must have been at Greta's house. I felt my face burning with shame and fear over what we had done.

"You could hear them crunching, there were so many of them," Greta went on. She seemed to relish telling the details. "And you should have seen my grandmother. She was out there swinging her cane around."

Suddenly, I had a terrible feeling that I was going to laugh. The more I tried not to, the more I felt I would. I tried to control myself by saying something that turned out to be pretty lame.

"Were any of the caterpillars saved?"

I could hardly get the last word out before I was in convulsions on the floor. This set off Greta, and her laughs came in long shrieks. The two of us laughed so hard we hurt. We laughed so long we almost wet our pants. Our gasps and snorts brought her grandmother downstairs to ask what was the matter with us. This just set us off again. I thought we would never stop; I thought we would die laughing.

That was the beginning of a great friendship.

CHAPTER
TWO

Why do grown-ups think they can talk over your head? When my mother and her friends gossip, they think I don't understand what they're saying, because they talk all around a subject instead of using plain words. Or they don't finish a sentence and then give each other meaningful looks. Well, it doesn't take a genius to fill in the blanks—I've learned how to figure out what goes in blanks from taking school tests.

That's how I happened to learn about the Mallards being broke. My mother was talking about it with a friend in a secretive way. I didn't let on that I got it, though. That's part of the game. (Kids don't tell that they can catch on to adults' scrambled messages, otherwise an important source of information would dry up.)

What I pieced together was that Mr. Mallard had been on unemployment for so many weeks that his benefits had finally run out. Also, the farm implement plant, where he used to work, was probably never going to open again. My mother's friend thought the family would probably have to move to another town so he could find a job.

This really worried me, but I didn't let on. I had been friends with Greta for four years by then, and I never thought about the possibility of our ever being separated. Not that we don't have other friends. Greta is close to a girl named Nicole, who goes to her school. I don't like Nicole much. She is very athletic, and I'm not. Whenever the three of us get together, she wants to shoot basketballs or jump rope double Dutch. I end up having to turn the rope because I always miss on the first jump.

I have a special friend, too, named Dawn. Her mother and mine are close, so I see a lot of her. She is almost a year older than I and really knows how to dress. Sometimes our mothers arrange for us to stay all night at each other's houses.

But Greta is my closest friend in the world, and I was shocked when I heard that her family was in trouble. Of course, I knew her father had been laid off several times, but he always got called back to work after a few weeks or months. And Greta had never let on that they didn't have enough money. I wondered if she even knew it. Now, if I heard right, the plant was going to shut down for good.

It was summer, and our family was getting ready to leave for the lake. Every August we spend four weeks at our cabin up north. My mother doesn't really like it there, but my dad does. He's a fisherman, and he's teaching my brothers how to cast with spinners and things.

I started to worry that Greta might move away before I got back and that we would never see each other again. I didn't tell anyone about my fear, and I certainly didn't tell Greta, since she might not even know that her family was having money troubles.

"What's the matter with you, Lindsay?" my mom asked me one day. "You've been moping around here like a sick cat. Why don't you call up Dawn and ask her to come over?"

"She's at her swimming lesson."

"Well, go over to Greta's then."

That was when the idea hit me. Why not invite Greta to come to the lake with us? My mom seemed taken aback when I asked her about it, but she didn't say no. It would be up to my dad, anyway.

That night I overheard them talking about it.

"Seems like a good idea, Kay. The boys and I fish together, and she probably needs a friend to play with. Besides, it'll be one less mouth for the Mallards to feed."

It was settled then.

On the day we left, Greta arrived with a suitcase tied up with rope. In it were the clothes her mother had made her. They didn't look like they were from The

Gap, but they were cute. We all piled in our car and were off for what turned out to be the best vacation of my life.

Greta and I swam and went out in our boat and hiked to the post office, but the most fun we had was just poking around on the beach. Greta was a genius when it came to finding things.

"Take a look at this. I guess they're eggs, but their shells are all dented and soft."

"They look like ruined Ping-Pong balls," I said. "Hey, there are a whole lot more under the sand."

Together, we dug up twenty-four of the strange eggs and put them into an empty bait bucket that my father had left on the dock.

"Let's take them up to the house and see if anything hatches out of them."

The eggs, we decided, should be kept in sand, since that was where they had been laid. So we poured a lot of the stuff into the bucket, which made it quite heavy. Between the two of us, though, we managed to lug it to our cabin yard.

It took a few days for something to happen.

"Hey, come here," Greta called to me one afternoon. "One of the eggs is moving."

"And this one is splitting," I pointed out.

You couldn't say it was cracking, because the shell was too leathery to break like that. We watched some yellow fluid ooze out. What could be inside? Soon another one began to move slightly, and its soft shell split. Then yellow fluid oozed out of it.

"I hope we aren't hatching baby dinosaurs," I said.

"Oh, I hope we are!" Greta almost shrieked with excitement over the idea. "That would be really great!"

I don't know how long it took, maybe a half hour, before a tiny clawed foot protruded from the slit and began to wave.

"Well, that does look like it could be a tiny dinosaur paw," Greta said.

"Paw! Did you say paw?"

We both laughed.

"I can see the headline now: GIRLS FIND AND HATCH FIRST DINOSAUR EGGS IN MILLIONS OF YEARS. We'll be famous!" Greta said.

Of course, we didn't really believe we had found dinosaur eggs. That's how we talk. When my dad hears us carry on, he says we have "the gift of whimsy," whatever that means. It's just our way of having fun.

After an hour the so-called dinosaur paw stopped waving at us, and the yellow fluid along the slit dried up. I thought the baby whatever-it-was must have died.

"I think we'd better peel this egg," I said.

Greta did it. Slowly, she stripped away the soft shell covering. It was kind of like opening a present, because we had no idea what was inside.

"Maybe it's a snake," I said to scare her.

"Snakes don't have feet."

"Well, a lizard then."

Greta was unflappable. That's the word my mother uses to describe her. It means a person who doesn't get all worked up, no matter what is happening.

When Greta had finished peeling the egg, she cupped both hands around it so that I couldn't see what she held. Then she made me wait a few seconds until she was ready to open one hand and present it with a "Ta dah!"

"Oh, a turtle, a turtle! Oh, how adorable! Let me hold it."

For the rest of the day, we hatched turtles. Each one had a tiny sac attached to its underside, which we later learned contained food. We only had to peel two more. The rest of the babies were able to work their own way out of their shells. All they needed to do was get *both* front feet into the slit before the yellow fluid dried up. Then, after a long struggle, they pushed themselves out the rest of the way.

In the middle of all this, we transferred the un-hatched eggs to a big tub, used for rinsing out bathing suits, and then dragged it out of the hot sun. This kept the yellow ooze from drying up so fast. When that happened, the babies got glued to the eggshell and couldn't make any more progress without our help.

One baby needed to be peeled out because its shell

had split open on the wrong side. After a while, we realized that the foot waving at us was a hind one. Turtles need to use their front feet to pull themselves out.

It felt wonderful helping to bring twenty-four turtles into the world. That night at dinner Greta described what we had done. Well—the response we got nearly knocked us off our chairs.

"Turtles!" my brother Will shouted. "They've gone and hatched turtles, Dad."

"What's wrong with turtles?" Mom asked quietly.

"They ruin the fishing," Will said.

"Is that true, Charles?" my mother asked my dad.

"Well, they don't help it," he acknowledged.

"Where are these turtles? I'm going to destroy them," Will announced.

"No, you're not!" I shouted back at him.

"Yes, I am," he said.

I burst into tears and ran from the table.

"Come back here, Lindsay. You haven't been excused," my dad said.

I pretended I didn't hear him and ran into my bedroom and slammed the door.

"You're excused, Greta, if you want to go with her," my mom said.

We could hear my brothers and dad discussing the "turtle situation" through the thin cabin walls. They said that the turtles we had hatched were the kind that eat baby fish, and the lake was being ruined by these turtles.

Greta whispered that she wasn't sure that was true. She had kept a pet turtle in an aquarium once, and it hadn't eaten anything at all, not turtle food, not flies, nothing. I wondered if we could make a case for saving the turtles, based on her expert opinion. My dad is a lawyer and he always likes to hear us kids present our cases. First, though, we would have to line up our facts, otherwise he would demolish us.

Just then my dad knocked on the door and said that I should stop crying and come out; the boys weren't going to be allowed to destroy the turtles. We would find some other solution in a day or two.

This gave us time to research turtles and see if we could come up with a case. The next morning we hiked down to the Ike Walton camp and asked to see the proprietor, Lanny Black.

Lanny Black is a skinny man who lives at the lake all year round and sells sporting goods and bait. In winter he rents cabins to duck hunters. If anyone ought to know whether or not turtles eat, and if so, what, he should.

"Depends on what kind of turtle you're talking about," he told us. "Some eat plants and insects. Others eat fish, frogs, even ducks."

"How would we know which kind we have?" I asked.

"What does it look like?"

Neither of us could describe the turtles except to say that they were babies.

"Well, I hope you haven't gone and hatched snapping turtles up there. This lake doesn't need more of them."

We decided to end the interview then and there, before he got too interested in our turtles. Just as we were leaving, though, he handed us a field guide.

"Here, you might be able to identify your turtles from this. You can return it tomorrow."

We ran all the way back to the cabin and compared our turtles to pictures in the book. It didn't take long to match them up with a painting of a baby snapping turtle. It was the only turtle in the book with a tail as long as its shell.

"Wow, we've got the worst kind," I said. "Let's see what the book says they eat."

"I don't know why you say they're the worst kind," Greta said. "Even if they eat fish, so do we. I can't see what's so bad about that."

"I was only thinking about winning our case," I answered. "I don't think snapping turtles are bad animals just because they eat the same things we do. I don't even think caterpillars are bad just because they ate up your grandmother's garden."

The memory of that event sent us into gales of laughter. When we finally calmed down, I got back to the book.

"Here it says that snapping turtles eat crayfish,

snails, insects, fish, frogs, salamanders, reptiles, birds, mammals, and aquatic plants. Gee, with a diet like that, we ought to be able to argue that they won't be eating *many* fish."

"That's good," Greta agreed.

"We could also make the case that they *control* snakes. My mom would go for that."

We tried to think of more arguments, but those were all we could come up with. Still, I had the feeling that we had overlooked something important. It didn't seem right that our turtles were going to be destroyed just because they ate things that people wanted to keep for themselves. The book said the snapping turtle had lived on earth for millions and millions of years, long before people were here. Somehow that seemed important to me, though I couldn't see how to present it as an argument.

That evening my dad asked if I wanted to discuss the turtle situation. I was as ready as I would ever be, so I said okay. Of course he expected to do all the talking. I hadn't told him yet that I was preparing a case. Just as I expected, he began by pointing out that we had to be considerate of the summer people who came here to fish; they wouldn't want a lake full of snapping turtles.

When I answered that I was ready to present the other side, he looked surprised.

"Snapping turtles have to live beside and in water," I began, "and *we* don't. We can live anywhere. We come to this lake because we like it. Turtles live here because it's been their home for millions and millions of years, and they *can't* live anyplace else. If we kill everything that eats what we eat, what will the earth be like? Think of that!"

I left out the arguments about controlling snakes and the question of how many fish the turtles actually might eat. But what I said seemed to go over with my dad.

"I think I'd like you on my law team," was all he said.

That night Greta and my dad and I went together in the boat to the lake outlet. There we released twenty turtles. Four had already made their escape. They were last seen moving off our beach into my brothers' fishing water.

CHAPTER THREE

After such a great summer I didn't feel like going back to school. In fact, it was a real letdown for the first few weeks. Then I got a part in the Thanksgiving play, and things began to pick up. We rehearsed every afternoon. I could hardly find time to see Greta, but then again, she was busy too. She had made it all the way to the state spelling finals by spelling *entomology* correctly. (It means the study of insects.) Only Greta would know how to spell that word. My dad commented that her early interest in caterpillars had finally paid off.

One evening I got an urgent phone call from Greta. She wouldn't tell me what was up; she would only say she wanted me to come over right away. My mom was fitting my costume on me at that moment, so I was stuck for a while and had to wonder and worry about what was on Greta's mind. I hoped she wasn't going to tell me that she was moving away. Her dad was still unemployed. A lot of people were. Every night I heard on the news that there weren't any manufacturing jobs left in our town.

When, at last, I was released from all the pins, I ran the two blocks to her house and banged on the door. Immediately, she flung it open.

"I saw you coming," she said. "Follow me."

I was relieved to see that she didn't look at all upset as she led me down to the basement.

"Wait till you see what I found," she said, carefully opening a cardboard box that had holes punched in its sides. "Take a look!"

I peered into the box, which at first seemed to hold nothing but torn-up newspaper and a piece of bark. Then I began to notice that the bark was actually feathers. Finally, I realized I was looking at a tiny owl.

"Oh, where did you find it?"

"Beside the road that winds through Red Rock Park. It must have flown against the windshield of the car in front of us, but the people just drove on. My dad stopped and let me pick it up and bring it home. Now I'm trying to find out what's wrong with it so I can help it."

"I never saw a live owl before. I didn't even know they came in such a small size. What kind is it?"

"I don't know. What do you think I should feed it?"

"It doesn't look very hungry to me," I commented.

The little owl was lying on its side with its toes curled and its eyes closed.

"I hope it lives," I said. "Do you think it's cold?"

The Mallards hadn't turned on their heat yet, even though the late fall nights had become quite chilly.

"I'll get a hot water bottle," Greta said, and dashed up the stairs. She returned a few minutes later with a plastic shampoo bottle filled with warm water and wrapped in a towel. With great care, she lifted the bird and placed it on this warm bed.

"Do you think it's a baby?" I asked.

"No. Birds don't have babies in the fall, that much I know. It has to be some tiny species of owl."

"Well, the only kind of owl I can think of is the hoot owl, and they're huge."

"Maybe it's a screech owl. How big are they?"

"I bet it's a screech owl." I had seen one on a TV show, and Greta's bird looked a lot like the one in the film. I remembered that it had little tufts on its head too. Of course, you can't tell about size from television. Once I saw a film on African mole rats and I thought they were as big as gophers. Later, when I saw some in a zoo, they turned out to be the size of grubs. It was a real disappointment.

We gazed at the bird for a long time without speaking, just hoping it would wake up. Finally, Greta's mother called us upstairs.

"You girls have school tomorrow," she said. "And Greta leaves for the state spelling contest in the afternoon. I think you'd better call it a night."

Suddenly, Greta jumped up.

"Oh, I forgot," she said.

"You forgot the contest?" her mother asked.

"No, I forgot why I called Lindsay over here."

Then she turned to me. "I won't be able to look after the owl until I get back—which will probably be pretty quick, since I don't expect to survive the first round. Anyway, will you take care of it for the next couple of days while I'm away?"

She didn't have to ask me twice. Even if I didn't know a thing about caring for sick birds, I wanted to try.

"Should I take it home with me?" I asked.

"You can if you want. Or you can take care of it over here. I'll look after it in the morning, and then my dad can let you in after school. He's home all day."

Since I didn't know how my folks would react to having a sick owl as an overnight guest, I agreed to Greta's plan.

That night I couldn't sleep, wondering if the little bird was going to make it. The next day at school I could hardly wait for lunch period. Instead of eating, I went to the library to look for a book on owls. Greta had phoned in the morning to say that the patient had opened its eyes and was sitting up. It would need to be fed. But what?

Our school librarian, Mrs. Freed, helped me find a field guide on birds. It contained pictures and descriptions of twelve different kinds of owls. Most of them I could rule out immediately as being too big. Only the boreal owl, the saw-whet owl, the burrowing owl, and the screech owl were the right size to be our bird. And of these four, only the screech owl had ear tufts. That was it, then.

There wasn't much information on the bird's habits. Mostly, the book told about color and distribution, and there was only one line about food, saying that screech owls eat a lot of flying insects and mice. Now how was I supposed to feed this bird? There weren't any moths flying around in November. And as for mice, I didn't think we had any of those in our house.

Then Mrs. Freed gave me another book, this one on raptors. Eagles and hawks and owls all belong to the raptor group. All these birds eat meat and have hooked beaks and sharp talons, so that they can seize and kill birds, fish, and small animals. When a raptor pounces on a victim, its curved talons sink in and lock in place. It's impossible for a raptor to withdraw its talons until the prey stops struggling. Then the bird will fly to a perch and begin to tear its meal apart with its beak. Whew!

Now I was *sure* I wouldn't be able to feed the owl, but I couldn't just let it starve. The book said that owls and hawks need to eat every day, so they can keep up their strength for more hunting. Well, maybe the bird

Greta found could be set free to do its own killing, because, even if I knew how, I sure didn't want to hunt and kill mice. My hope was that there was nothing much wrong with it, and that Greta wouldn't be mad at me if I decided to set it free.

Mrs. Freed suggested that I try feeding it raw hamburger, instead of mice, but the book said that owls need to eat the fur and claws and bones of their prey. Afterward, they throw up some of these indigestible parts in little wads, called castings.

By the time I finished school that day, I was worried sick. I headed directly for Greta's house right after school. (We didn't have play practice in the afternoon because we were doing a dress rehearsal that night.) Her dad let me in.

"I've looked in on the bird," he said. "I think its wing feathers are broken."

That was a lot of words to come out of his mouth. He never was the talkative type, and, lately, he had been what you might call mute. He just sat around looking tired.

I ran down the stairs and peered into the box. The little bird hissed, fell on its back, and showed me its sharp talons. Naturally, I didn't put my hand in the box, but just talked softly to it.

"Don't be scared," I said over and over. "I'm not going to hurt you."

After a while, the owl sat up and began flopping around the box. I could see that something was definitely wrong. Nearly all of the feathers on one of its wings were broken off. This little owl couldn't possibly fly on one wing. So much for setting it free. I would have to find food for it. Oh, for those caterpillars now! Or better still, the moths and butterflies that they had turned into. I climbed the stairs and confronted Mr. Mallard.

"Do you have any hamburger?" I asked.

"You hungry?" he asked.

"No, it's for the bird."

"For the bird?" He seemed taken aback.

"Yes, the bird has to eat something now."

He moved toward the refrigerator and looked inside. I could see there wasn't much there. Mrs. Mallard had gone to Springfield with Greta and left two plates of food, one for her husband and one for Albert. I watched him take the wax paper off the plates and look at what she had made. On each plate was a slice of meat loaf, a potato, and some carrots and peas.

"Here," he said, handing me the slice of meat loaf.

It was nice of him to offer it, but since it was already cooked, it probably wouldn't be any good for an owl. When I explained this to him, he asked what other food, besides raw meat, the bird would eat.

"Mice," I said.

"Mice?"

"Mice."

After a long silence he said that maybe we could trap some in the garage. He thought he had seen some droppings there.

I didn't like the idea of trapping mice, but Mr. Mallard was being really nice, and I didn't want to offend him by telling him how I felt. I never like to see anything hurt. Now, though, I couldn't think of what else we could do. So we set three traps with peanut butter bait and placed them in the garage.

"When will they come?" I asked.

"After dark."

I went home to my own dinner and tried not to think about the poor dead chicken lying on my plate. Life is really not too nice, when you consider the problem of eating.

Dress rehearsal went okay that night, and the next morning I got up really early and banged on the Mallards' door.

"Come on in," Mr. Mallard called out. "I've got good news for you."

"We caught a mouse?"

"Two."

It was funny how I felt about this news. I was glad for the owl, but sorry for the mice—especially when I saw their poor little squashed bodies. Mr. Mallard took them out of the traps and handed them to me. Ugh! I held them by their tails and looked away as I carried

them down the basement stairs. I began to wonder what I was doing there. When I uncovered the box, it hissed at me. Well, at least it was still alive.

"See what I brought you?" I said in a soft voice. "You're going to like these."

I dangled one of the mice in front of the owl, but it pressed its beak into its chest and backed away. When I pushed the mouse toward the owl's beak, its horns flew up.

"Don't tell me I killed this poor little mouse for nothing! You'd better take it."

The bird showed no interest in my offering. Well, I couldn't wait all day. I had to get to school. So I left the dead mice in the box and went upstairs.

"What happened?" Mr. Mallard asked.

"It didn't take them. I left them in the box."

"It'll eat."

"When is Greta coming home? Did they call?"

"Yep. She's still in the contest."

That was good news for her, but I sure wished she was around to share my misery over what her dad and I were doing.

At school Mrs. Freed stopped me in the hall and asked how things were going with the bird. When I told her I had trapped mice for it, she acted as if that was okay.

"It's a wild creature. It must eat what nature intends it to eat. You did the right thing," she said.

Our play was going to be held that night, so we didn't have a rehearsal in the afternoon. After school, I went directly to see the owl. When I lifted the lid, it didn't hiss or anything.

At first, I couldn't see any dead mice, but that didn't mean that the owl had eaten them. They could be buried in the torn-up newspaper. I noticed that the paper was dirty and needed changing. I hunted around the basement, found another empty box, then tried to lift the owl out of the mess and put it into the holding box. It was easy to catch because, even though it tried to flap its wings, it wasn't able to fly.

After securing the bird in the empty box, I dumped the dirty newspaper into a trash bin, taking care to look for any mice that might be buried in it. One fell out whole, and I picked it up and laid it on the floor. The other one wasn't there. I pawed through the newspaper several times to make sure I hadn't missed it. It was definitely not there. I felt elated. The bird had eaten the mouse! I ran upstairs to ask Mr. Mallard for some clean newspaper and to tell him the good news.

"One of the mice is gone."

He grinned.

"Do you have any newspaper?" I asked.

"What for?" he asked.

"To tear up for the bird box."

"Is that a good idea?"

"I don't know. That's how Greta had it."

"I'll take a look."

We went into the basement, and Mr. Mallard didn't even glance at the box. Instead, he sorted through some torn screens that were stacked behind the furnace.

"I'll do something with these," he muttered to himself.

"Should I put the bird back into its own box?" I asked.

"Just leave it," he replied.

I didn't know whether to go or stay.

Finally, I said, "The dead mouse is on the floor here."

"Okay," was all he answered.

But as I started up the stairs, he called after me, "Good luck in the play tonight."

"Thanks," I said. "See you tomorrow."

I felt a big load was off my mind. Greta was going to be happy to come home and find the bird was eating. I couldn't wait to see her face when I told her how her dad and I had found a way to feed it. Now all I had to worry about was remembering my lines, hardly a big deal after what I had been through.

CHAPTER
FOUR

The cage that Mr. Mallard built for the owl was wonderful. It was made out of eight wooden-framed screens, which he had stored behind the furnace. Now they had found an important use.

The whole cage measured about four feet long, four feet high, and two feet wide. One screen served as the floor. Two screens, standing upright at each end, supported a roof, which was removable. The long sides were made of two screens, set on their sides and stacked on top of each other. On top of the floor, he had put a piece of composition board, lined with newspaper, which could be slipped in and out of a slot that was cut out of one end of the cage. The purpose of this was to make cleaning easy.

He seemed satisfied with what he had made, although he didn't say anything. He just grinned at my reaction to it. I was so pleased that I jumped up and down, like those people who win prizes on TV game shows. My dad says they are told to act that way, and that it isn't dignified to get so excited over money. I guess it's okay to get excited over a great owl cage, though.

Mr. Mallard had built a shelf inside the cage, which was made out of a thick slab of bark. The owl would feel right at home, perched on bark—just as if it were on the branch of a real tree. From another slab of bark, he had created a ramp so that the owl could walk or hop up to the shelf and down to the floor whenever it wanted to. This walking ramp was important since the bird couldn't fly up or down. Finally, he had enlarged the hole of an old birdhouse, which he then had set at one end of the shelf, so the owl could go inside when it wanted privacy.

I was sure the little owl would feel much more comfortable in this cage than in a cardboard box. It sat on the bark shelf, bobbed up and down, and made a chirring sound at the leftover dead mouse beside it. Every once in a while, it leaned forward and stretched its wings. I watched as long as I could, hoping to see it eat the mouse, but, finally, I had to leave for school.

I thought about the owl all day. It needed a name, but I thought Greta ought to choose it, since she was the one who found the bird. It was going to need a steady supply of mice, and I sure hoped that the Mallards' garage was well stocked with them. If not, what would we do? I wondered if the broken wing feathers would grow back so it could fly again. If they did, would we set it free or keep it as a pet?

That afternoon and for the next two days, I was still in charge of the owl. Greta had lasted through every round and had gone to the finals and won first prize in spelling for the entire state. It was so exciting! She got her picture in the paper, and the whole town was proud of her. Even my dad was impressed.

"She's a smart kid. Maybe she'll get a scholarship to a good college."

The afternoon she came home, I was waiting at her house. My mom had sent over a cake with red icing that read CONGRATULATIONS TO OUR CHAMPION SPELLER— only all the words were purposely misspelled. We ate cake and talked and laughed about all the funny things that happened to her during the contest. I told her about our school play. One boy in the cast didn't listen for his cue to come onstage, and I had to repeat my line four times, each time louder, until he finally heard it. By the time he made his entrance, the whole audience was laughing.

The main thing we talked about, though, was the owl. Greta was so happy with the cage her father built. She said it was better than winning the spelling contest. Together we watched the little bird climb up and down the ramp, and even saw it eat a dead mouse. That was a first, even for me. It held the critter with its feet and tore off the poor thing's head. Then after bolting the head down, it picked at the body until there was nothing left of it.

All this seemed shocking, especially to Greta, because she hadn't been through the process of reading books, setting traps, and becoming hardened to what it takes to keep an owl alive, as I had. But I found it hard to watch too.

"Well, we eat meat," Greta finally said. "Only, first, somebody else—the butcher, I guess—has to cut off the head of the chicken or the cow so that we don't have to see it looking at us."

Greta had a way of putting things.

Of course, the word got around pretty fast that we had a screech owl, and all the kids in the neighborhood came to see it. Even my brothers, Will and George, arrived to take a look.

"It kind of reminds me of a little cat with wings," George said.

"How can you stand the stink?" Will asked.

I didn't think Troll smelled. Troll is the name we gave the owl. Actually, it was the cage that stank, but only when it needed cleaning. Troll made droppings from his back end and coughed up castings from his front end, so it wasn't easy keeping the Castle spotless. "Castle" was the name we gave Troll's cage.

Troll's castings consisted of wads of mouse fur and

tiny mouse bones and even teeth, which he couldn't digest. Even so, these parts were necessary for him to eat. Otherwise, he would have trouble digesting the meat part of his food and might get sick and die.

It was fun to watch people's different reactions to Troll. Nicole offered Greta anything she owned in trade for him. I didn't worry for one second that Greta would take her up on it, even though Nicole has a lot of expensive athletic gear, including a twelve-speed bicycle and a new pair of figure skates.

My friend Dawn, on the other hand, said she thought that Troll looked like a beautiful feather muff. I didn't like that comparison.

Greta's brother, Albert, wanted to know why we called the bird a he, when we didn't even know if it was a male. That was a good question, since male and female screech owls look and act the same.

"We call it 'he,' because we named it Troll, and trolls are always he's—at least, I think so," Greta answered.

Over the next few days, visitors filed in and out of Greta's basement. And over the next few nights, Greta and I succeeded in trapping every last mouse in the Mallards' garage. When we found our traps empty two mornings in a row, we knew we would have to do something fast.

"Now what will we feed Troll?" we asked each other.

"We could try raw meat, like Mrs. Freed once suggested," I said.

"What about the fur? Troll needs to eat fur."

"Fur? Fur? That's it! I know where we can get some fur to stick into hamburger."

It seemed a perfect solution. My mom had a mink coat that she hardly ever wore. We could snip just a little off the inside, somewhere. She'd never notice it.

We ran to my house, raided the freezer of hamburger meat, and defrosted it in the microwave. Then we got my mom's coat out of the closet and clipped a little patch from under the cuff. We pressed this onto a chunk of meat and ran back to Greta's.

"I just hope Troll eats this," Greta said. "Otherwise, he's a goner."

We placed the wad of fur and hamburger beside him on the shelf, but Troll reacted to it as if it wasn't even food. He bobbed his head up and down and from side to side, as if trying to see it from every angle. He made a chittering sound. He closed one eye.

"Let's lift him out and hold it up to his beak," Greta said.

This wasn't the first time Troll had been out of his cage. Sometimes one of us would hold him while the other cleaned the Castle. To get him to perch, all we had to do was press a finger behind his feet, and he would back right onto it.

This time Troll perched on my finger, while Greta

put the wad of hamburger on a wooden paint stick and pushed it against the side of his beak. To our surprise, he grabbed it and gobbled it down.

"Man, he's hungry!" Greta said.

For the next two feedings, due to a continuing mouse shortage, we fed Troll mink-coated meatballs. Then the boom fell. With the first really cold day of the season, my mom discovered that "moths" had gotten into her coat, and she whisked it off to the cleaners. There it was treated with chemicals to prevent further damage. I was afraid the cleaners would tell her that it wasn't a moth problem at all, and then she would begin asking questions, but that didn't happen. Quite the opposite! The cleaners told her that moths were definitely eating the coat, and that she was lucky to have found out about it before they did "conspicuous harm."

After that close call, we had to think of some other way to provide Troll with the roughage he needed.

"What about our own hair?" Greta wondered.

"I don't know. Do you think it would make Troll sick? It should be animal hair."

"We're animals," Greta said.

Suddenly, I had a brainstorm.

"I've got it! We'll use dog hair!"

I leapt to my feet. We could harvest it all from one dog, McGregor, the shelty that lives next door to us. He sheds a lot, and every time I invite him in for a visit, Marie has to get out the vacuum cleaner. McGregor could provide us with an endless supply of exactly what we needed.

Greta was elated with the idea. That afternoon we waited at my house and watched out the window until our neighbors let McGregor out. Then we called him inside and played rough games with him so that he would roll all over the floor. When Marie came in, she had a fit.

"I just vacuumed in here, and I'm not going to do it again, young lady. That's your job this time."

I acted sorry and got out the vacuum cleaner.

"Change the bag first so the dog hair won't get all mixed in with dirt," Greta warned.

Our plan worked perfectly. We got a wad of dog hair as big as a wig.

Now that we had the problem of Troll's food supply worked out, I started thinking about his injury. Would he ever fly again? I read somewhere that owls make no wing sounds when they sail out of a tree after their prey. It made me sad to think Troll might never again enjoy a silent flight through the woods in the middle of the night. That's when owls hunt. Greta seemed surprised when I mentioned all of this to her.

"Oh, he'll get better," she assured me. "We just have to wait for new feathers to grow in."

"How do you know they will?" I asked.

"Of course they will. Birds molt old feathers and grow new ones all the time."

I wasn't sure this was true. I had never seen a bird flopping around on the ground without any feathers.

"How do they get their food after they've molted?" I asked.

"Oh, they don't molt all at once, just a feather at a time. Anyway, I know new feathers do grow in. You remember that parakeet I kept for Nicole when her family went on vacation? Its wing feathers had been clipped, so it couldn't fly around her room and bump into things. After a while, though, they all grew back, and it could fly again."

This was certainly good news. Troll would get better! All we had to worry about was keeping him fed.

"How long does it take?" I asked.

"That's what I don't know. We'll just have to wait and see."

As the days grew shorter and the weather grew colder, people started talking about Christmas presents. I decided to give Greta a book on screech owls and asked my mom to drive me to a mall on the outskirts of town. There are three bookstores there. One of them would surely have the kind of book that I was looking for, something with good owl information and color pictures.

It snowed the Saturday we shopped, and we had to wear our high boots. My mom went to a department store while I checked the nature sections of all three bookstores. But as it turned out, I couldn't find a thing.

I did look at a book on raptors that had a section about owls, but I didn't buy it. Who would want to pay a high price for a book that devoted only one little paragraph to the screech owl? I read everything it had to say while I was standing there, and that wasn't anything Greta and I didn't already know.

I would have counted this shopping trip a total waste of time if it hadn't been for what happened next. As I headed back to the car, I noticed a bunch of people standing about, looking at the ground. Curiosity got the better of me, and I made a detour to see what had caught everyone's attention. It's a good thing I did! What I saw lying in the snow was a strange-looking bird.

"Is it alive?" I asked a woman in the crowd.

"Seems so, but I nearly stepped on it."

Some of the people started to leave, and I realized that no one intended to do anything more than take a quick look at the bird. Only the woman who spoke seemed at all concerned.

"It'll get run over if it's left here," she said. "Maybe we should tell a store manager about it."

Right then and there I knew I had to take the bird home, but I didn't say so. Instead, I told the woman that I would find a store manager and ask him to come out.

"Oh, would you, dear?" she said. "Well, I can leave, then."

As soon as she got into her car and drove off, I picked up the bird and carried it to our car, where my mom was waiting for me with the motor running and the heater on. She didn't bat an eye when she saw what I had in my arms. All she did was laugh.

"So you found something better than a book to give Greta."

When we got home and laid the bird on the kitchen floor, my dad pronounced it a grebe. He said he had seen such birds swimming on our lake.

"That bird may be easier to feed than your owl," he said. "It eats fish, which, I suppose, we can buy for it." He turned to my mom.

"You can get smelts at the fish store, can't you, Kay?"

My mom nodded.

I was surprised that my parents seemed so accepting of the bird, and I decided to "quickly embrace my opportunity." That's my dad's phrase. "Always be quick to embrace the opportunities that come your way," he says. So, following his advice, I went directly to the phone.

"You'll never believe what happened, Greta. Another bird has landed on us. It's a grebe, and I found it nearly frozen in a parking lot this morning. Oh, and in case your parents give you a hard time about our newest patient, just tell them that this bird was heaven-sent."

CHAPTER
FIVE

My dad says that grebes live on our lake, but I've never seen one. Of course, he sits in a boat for hours at a time, waiting for fish to bite. It's really not so strange that he happened to notice this funny-looking little waterbird.

At first I thought the grebe had lost all its tail feathers. But when I found a drawing of it in our encyclopedia, I saw that it didn't have much of a tail to begin with. The bird's problem might have been ice on its wing feathers. I've heard of airplanes crashing due to wing ice, but I never imagined such a thing could happen to a bird.

When Greta arrived, we talked about what to do with the latest arrival to our bird hospital. How to keep it? Together we read that this kind of bird swims about all the time and never comes up on land. Even its babies are born on floating nests made out of weeds and reeds. From almost the minute they are out of their shells, they climb onto their mother's back and ride around. When she dives after fish, they just hang on and go under with her.

"It wouldn't use a perch, I guess," Greta said.

The bird had revived by now, but it still seemed weak. When we tipped it upright, it wasn't able to stand on its legs.

"Do you know what I think?" I said. "If this bird likes water so much, why not let it float around in a bathtub?"

Greta hesitated.

"Don't you like the idea?" I asked.

"I do, but we only have one bathtub in our house. I can't put a bird in it, or we won't have one for ourselves. Of course, Albert would love that."

"Well, we have plenty of bathrooms here, and we never take baths all at the same time. So why not keep the bird here?"

The only problem was convincing my folks to go along with our plan, which, to my surprise, was not hard at all.

"You can't use Marie's or our bathrooms," my mom said. "And since the boys don't have a tub in theirs, I guess you'll have to give up your own."

Greta and I ran upstairs and filled my tub with luke-warm water. Grebes, we found out later, live in lakes that are pretty cool, but we didn't think about that at the time. Anyway, the warm water didn't do it any harm. In fact, it may have liked the heat, after having its wings frozen.

Still, the first thing the bird did when we placed it in the tub scared us to death. For a couple of seconds it sat on the surface, but then it started to sink. It went straight down, just like a submarine, until even its head was underwater. We just looked at each other. Then Greta cried out, "This bird sinks! Are you sure it's a grebe?"

While she hung over the tub and supported it above water with her hands, I raced downstairs, two steps at a time, and grabbed the encyclopedia.

"It's a grebe, all right," I said, out of breath, as I shoved the book under her face. "It's a pied-billed grebe, if you want to know exactly what it is."

Greta had to agree that the bird in the picture was the bird in the tub. "Will you hold it for a minute, so that I can read more carefully?" she asked.

"Maybe it needs a floating nest or something," I suggested, as we traded places. "We could make one out of weeds—that is, if there are any weeds at this time of year."

Just then, my dad appeared at the door.

"How's it going, girls?"

"The bird sinks. We have to hold it up to keep it from drowning," I explained.

I was draped over the tub with my back to him and about to take my hands away to show what would happen, when he burst out laughing.

"I've seen them do that. Did it just scuttle itself like a sinking boat?"

"Yes, yes," Greta and I answered together.

"Oh, well, that's okay. They do that sometimes. I don't know how they manage it. They must squeeze all the air out of their feathers. Anyway, I don't think a grebe is likely to drown. They dive and swim underwater for long periods while they fish."

My dad's words were a great relief to us. I was surprised by them too. I had no idea he knew anything about birds, much less such an unusual one.

"Your mom's gone to the store to buy some smelts," he went on. "I think, after we've fed this critter, it can be on its way."

"On its way? Where is it going?" Greta asked.

My dad seemed surprised by her question.

"Wherever birds go in winter," he said. "I guess it was flying someplace when it fell."

"Maybe it can't fly," I said.

"Well, of course, we'll check that out first," he said. "We won't just send it off in the cold if it can't fly."

With that, he walked out of the room.

"I don't think it can fly, or it would be flapping around right now," Greta said under her breath. "Let go of it and see what happens."

No sooner did I release the bird than it dipped headfirst into the water and swam around the tub below the surface. When it bobbed up again, Greta and I had to laugh. At that moment, my mom came in with the smelts and threw some into the water. We waited for the grebe to find and eat them, but it didn't seem to know what they were.

"I don't suppose it's used to eating dead things," my mom said.

"Should we hold a smelt up to its beak?" I asked Greta.

"Why not?"

A pied-billed grebe's beak is not at all like a duck's or a goose's. It's small like a chicken's and has one dark stripe across the top of it. I held the bird steady, while Greta pressed one of the little fishes against its mouth. The grebe struggled free and shook its head.

"I'm going to force its mouth open," Greta said at last. "But first you'd better haul it out of the water, so you can get a good grip on it."

After some discussion, I tucked the bird under one arm, to keep its wings from flapping, and held its head with my opposite hand. Greta tried to pry the bird's mouth open, but without success. Then she hit on the idea of pinching the base of its beak with two fingers. This caused its mouth to fly open for a second, and after several tries, she managed to push a piece of smelt into its mouth. My dad and mom, who were watching, cheered as the grebe gulped it down.

"Now that it knows what a smelt is, why don't you just let it take the next piece," my mom suggested.

We tried this and it worked. The bird grabbed it. After we succeeded in getting one whole smelt into the grebe—a piece at a time—we put the bird back in the water and dangled a whole one in front of its bill. It snatched and ate it immediately.

"Your bird is going to be fine," my dad said. "We'll let it rest here tonight and release it in the morning."

To make our overnight guest feel at home, Greta and I placed potted ivy on a towel shelf above the tub. These hanging plants dropped all the way to the water and made a kind of curtain of leaves for the grebe to hide in. Even though the encyclopedia said that grebes do not come ashore, we also put my mom's bread board in the tub to act as a raft, just in case our grebe wanted something to climb up on. Then we turned out the lights and left it alone.

The next morning I woke up early and ran into the bathroom to see how it was doing. I found it hiding inside the dangling ivy, but it must have been awake for some time, because all the smelts we had left in the tub were gone. I offered it more, and it took them too.

Greta arrived right after breakfast, and we watched the bird swim among the vines until my dad came in and said, "I think this would be a good time to release our feathered sojourner."

Both of us felt sorry about this decision, but you don't argue with my dad, unless you've prepared your case. So we carried the bird to our backyard and placed it on the snow, which had frozen hard during the night. For some reason, the bird was still unable to stand on its

legs, maybe because they were placed so far back on its body. Its wings looked okay by now. Even so, when it flapped them, it didn't go anywhere. It just toppled over onto its beak.

"Something's wrong with it," Greta said.

"I think it just needs a little help gaining lift," my dad answered, picking it up and holding it high. "We'll just give it a toss." And with that, he threw the bird high in the air. For a moment, the grebe's wings fluttered like a butterfly's. Then it fell to the ground with a thud.

"Oh, did it hurt itself?" I cried out.

My dad assured me that the bird was just fine—even before he had picked it up and looked at it. But after one more unsuccessful toss, even *he* thought it would be best to bring the grebe back into the house. Once inside, he made a call to one of his country club friends, Pete Simon.

Pete Simon is a bird-watcher. He has looked at so many birds in this country that he had to make a trip to Australia last summer, just to see some that he didn't already know. Greta and I could hardly wait for my dad to finish his conversation with Mr. Simon and tell us what he had to say. I was sure that the grebe was injured in some way and needed to be taken to a bird doctor—that is, if there is such a thing. But Greta was not as worried as I was. She said any bird that is seriously hurt wouldn't eat like ours did. She had a point.

My dad took ages to wind up his conversation. He

even got onto other subjects, having nothing to do with birds, before he said good-bye. When at last he did, he turned to us and grinned.

"Simon says . . . " He paused there, waiting for us to get the joke. "Simon says," he finally continued, "that grebes can only take off from open water. They need a long runway, at that. They have to scoot across the surface of a pond or a lake, paddling their feet and flapping their wings as fast as they can, until they pick up enough speed to become airborne."

"There isn't any open water now," Greta said. "The pond in Red Rock Park has turned into a skating rink."

"That's right," my dad said. "That's why the grebe ended up where it did. It probably mistook that snowy lot for open water and tried to land there. Once it was grounded, it couldn't take off again."

I was relieved by this news. Glad, in fact.

"So it's not hurt," I said. "Well then, I guess we'll just have to keep it alive on a diet of smelts until spring."

"Nothing doing," my dad said. "You can be sure there will be a thaw long before spring. There always is. And this bird shouldn't be kept in captivity too long. It needs to find its way south."

For the next week, Greta and I watched the grebe swim about in the hanging ivy and eat the fish that we offered it. Sometimes it took a smelt right from our hands. And every day I listened to weather reports, hoping that the cold would last. I certainly didn't want to say good-bye to our little bird. I had really gotten to like it. I loved the way it bobbed up, unexpectedly, after a long swim underwater. And when it "scuttled itself," as my dad put it, even my brothers had to laugh.

Finally, though, the temperature began to climb until one day most of the snow and ice were gone.

"It's time," my dad said. "We'll let it go today after school."

I had hoped he would be too busy to notice the change in the weather. So had Greta. She felt as bad as I did at the thought of releasing the bird. It had become a kind of pet. And who would want to turn their pet loose, not knowing what would become of it? What if our grebe made the same mistake all over again and landed in another snowy parking lot? Would somebody else pick it up, and take it home and feed it? Or would it just die?

That day at school, I talked to our librarian about my worries.

"Not knowing what lies in store for the bird is truly hard," Mrs. Freed agreed. "On the other hand, a bath-tub is no place for a wild creature to live out its life. That grebe needs to explore a lake bottom, and hunt for its own food, and find a mate, and raise chicks. It won't be able to do any of those interesting things if you don't set it free. It will turn into nothing more than a rubber toy that floats in a bathtub."

I thought about what she said all day. I wanted her to be wrong, but I knew she was right.

That afternoon, Greta and my dad and I took the bird to Red Rock Park and put it in a marshy part of the pond. For a few minutes, it just sat in the weeds and did nothing at all. Maybe it was taking its bearings or something. At last, though, it paddled out into the open water and went under. For a long time, we didn't see it. Then Greta spied it when it popped up at the opposite end of the pond.

"It's probably fishing," my dad said.

Down it went again. We didn't know where to look for it next, so we kept scanning the pond. Finally, it surprised us by turning up right where we were standing.

I could have watched it forever, but, suddenly, the little grebe began flapping and running on top of the water. It ran the full length of the pond. And when it got to the far end, it sailed right up into the sky. I almost couldn't see its wings, they fluttered so fast. And then it was gone.

"It's heading south. That's a good bird," my dad said.

I had tears in my eyes, but not from the bird leaving. It was the cold weather that made my cry. Really.

"Make it to where you are trying to go," I called up to the empty sky.

"Right on," Greta shouted.

We didn't talk as we rode home, but I knew that I would never again come to Red Rock Park without remembering our grebe.

CHAPTER
SIX

I had just stopped worrying about Greta's moving away, when my dad let something drop that put me on edge again. I overheard him tell my mom that the Mallards might put their house up for sale.

"It isn't theirs, you know. It belongs to old Mrs. Mallard, who used to live with them. When she got sick, she moved back with her daughter. Now she's worse and requires full-time care. They should put her in a nursing home but they have no money, so the house is for sale. I don't know where Carl Mallard will go."

"That house can't be worth much in this market," my mom said. "Why doesn't Carl buy it from her?"

"Carl Mallard is flat broke. He hasn't had but a few part-time jobs for eight months now. And how much do you think Margaret makes working in a school office? Frankly, I don't know how they get by."

I tiptoed out of the adjoining room, ran upstairs,

and threw myself on my bed. For a long time, I lay there, staring at the ceiling, trying to figure out what I had heard. The world seemed out of control. Why should the Mallards have so much trouble? What did they ever do to deserve it? And what about us kids? Don't we have any say about what happens in our lives?

I wondered about Greta's silence. She never spoke to me about any of this, and I was her best friend! Didn't she know that what happened to her mattered to me? Or wasn't I important to her? What about our plan to live next door to each other someday and raise dogs and horses? And what about Troll, right now? What would become of him?

Lately, I had become his chief caretaker, because now Greta was baby-sitting most afternoons. Troll had gotten really used to me. Sometimes, I coaxed him on my finger and took him on a tour of the Mallards' house. I thought he must be bored, sitting in the Castle all the time with absolutely nothing to do.

That seemed to be Mr. Mallard's fate too. Most days he sat at home watching television, and when I let myself in, he hardly looked up to say hello. Even when I carried Troll right past him through the living room, he hardly noticed us. I knew he felt bad about not having a job, so I didn't take his unfriendliness to heart.

On days that it snowed, Troll and I had the house to ourselves. Mr. Mallard was off blowing snow from the driveways of people in the neighborhood. He even cleared ours, once, with his noisy, gas-powered snow blower. My dad said afterward that he had to give the man credit for picking up some money in this way, even though he seemed to have given up looking for steady employment.

On those days when the house was empty, I tried to teach Troll to fly again. His wing feathers were partway in by now, but he couldn't manage more than a few feet before he fell to the floor. I guess he needed to grow longer feathers and get back in practice.

One day Mrs. Freed suggested that I bring Troll to school for a show-and-tell. Greta gave her okay, but warned me about keeping the bird warm. I put him in a dog carrier that I borrowed from McGregor's owners, and my dad drove me right up to the school's back door.

I could never have guessed that Troll would make such a hit. The fourth, fifth, and sixth grades assembled in the library to hear me describe how Greta had found him, and how the two of us were taking care of him. Mrs. Freed had hung pictures of owls around the room. I explained what screech owls eat, and how much trouble we had feeding ours after we ran out of mice. One girl raised her hand and asked if it wasn't cruel to kill a *lot* of mice to feed *one* bird. That was a hard question.

"Well, I guess so, in a way, but this bird has to eat animals to live."

Then a boy shouted at the girl that since *she* ate meat, what was the big deal. The discussion got pretty hot, as you might imagine. Finally, Mrs. Freed asked for another question, which turned out to be: How long does it take for a bird's wing feathers to grow back? I said I didn't know the answer, but I was glad that they had started coming in.

"Won't you feel bad when they do and you have to set Troll free?"

"Don't you want to keep the bird?"

"Why don't you clip his other wing and make him a pet?"

Everyone was asking questions at the same time, and Mrs. Freed had to stand up and call for order. Then, when everyone was finally quiet, it was up to me to say something.

"I will feel bad when I have to let Troll go, but he'll be much happier when he's free. Even though he lives in a castle, he'd like a tree better. It's no fun having nothing to do, you know. I think he'd like to fly wherever he pleases and hunt for his own food."

After all the kids had filed out of the room, Mrs. Freed patted my shoulder and said that caring for birds had taught me a lot and that she was proud of me.

I guess my talk did go over well, judging from the things that came out of it. First, it made me kind of famous in our school. A lot of kids I hardly knew came up and wanted to talk to me. They wanted to bring in more animals for Greta and me to take care of—animals that they had found, but weren't allowed to keep at home. (But this led to some real trouble, which I will get to later.)

The first new addition to our menagerie turned out to be a baby red squirrel. I didn't know that baby squirrels are called pups, and that they are sometimes born as early as February. In fact, I didn't know much of anything about squirrels before Roy Reimers handed me a tiny pup with a skinny tail and big forehead. His dad had put traps in their attic and had killed the little squirrel's mother. Later that day, Roy's dad found the orphaned baby and called Roy to come look at it.

"We'll have to kill it too," his dad had told him. "It would be cruel to let it die a slow death from starvation. It has to have a mother to stay alive."

That's when Roy thought of me and Troll.

"I know someone who can raise a baby squirrel," he told his dad.

That's how Nutkin came to live with Greta and me.

As soon as Roy handed us the tiny baby, we saw that it was already weak from lack of food. Greta put it in a cardboard box filled with Kleenex. She added Troll's old heating pad, a plastic shampoo bottle filled with hot water. Then we warmed some milk and fed it to the little squirrel with an eyedropper. That's when Greta's mother stepped in.

"You're giving a baby squirrel milk that was made for a calf," she said. "Even human babies don't drink straight cow's milk. They have to be given special formulas."

Greta was not to be stopped, though.

"Something is better than nothing, and she has to eat right now," she insisted. "We'll find the right thing to give her later."

I trusted Greta. As my mom says about her, she has all the right instincts to survive. Now she was applying those instincts to save the baby squirrel.

For my part, I decided to research the subject. Since school was out for the day, I asked my mom to drive me to the public library. When I walked in, someone directed me to the children's room, where I found a lot of books on squirrels, but none that helped. All the animals in them wore clothes and talked to each other. Finally, I gave up and tried the adult section. When I asked a librarian where I could find books on squirrels, she pointed to the card catalog drawer and said that everything was listed there.

"Just write down the title and call number of the book you want, and if we have it, I'll get it for you."

There were so many listings for squirrels that I didn't know where to begin. So I went back to the car, where my mom was waiting.

"Why don't we call up a veterinarian?" she suggested. "I should think that one of them would know what to feed a baby squirrel. I'll phone next door and find out who McGregor's vet is."

That idea turned out to be the right solution. McGregor's vet told me to come right over and pick up

some Esbilac. He said he used this powder to mix formulas for orphan puppies and kittens, and that it would do just fine for a squirrel. He also gave me instructions on how often and how much to feed the baby—two ounces every three hours. Every three hours! How were we going to do that and go to school too?

When I arrived at Greta's with the Esbilac, it was already past time for Nutkin's second feeding, so we got right to it. I held the squirrel, while she mixed the formula and put some in the eyedropper. Then I fed the baby.

I have to say that Nutkin was cute enough to star in a Disney movie. She drank all the formula I gave her, except what she got on her face. I wiped that off with a Kleenex.

"My dad is going to have to help us with this one," Greta said. "He's home all the time now, anyway, so I'll show him how to do it."

That was the first time Greta had ever spoken to me about her dad's situation, and I wasn't about to press her to say more. Instead, I said, "It's lucky he can help," which sounded so dumb that I turned red in the face.

After that day we were really busy with Troll's needing hairy hamburgers and as many mice as we could catch, and Nutkin's many feedings. And we had to keep the Castle and the cardboard box clean, make sure the water in the shampoo bottle was nice and warm, and start Troll on a serious exercise program. Greta said his wing muscles would get to be like old, flabby rubber bands, unless he flapped them every day.

I loved exercising Troll. When he perched on my finger, I moved my arm up and down to make him open and close his wings. Whenever he made a serious attempt to fly, though, he always ended up on the floor.

One day we discovered a cricket in Greta's basement and offered it to Troll. For as long as we had had him, we had wanted to find a cricket or a cicada or a dragonfly to give him, because screech owls are supposed to love to eat big insects. But, of course, bugs don't come out in winter. Now, at last, we had one and we were eager to see how our owl would react to it.

First we carried Troll upstairs to Greta's bedroom and placed him on the floor. Then we released the cricket right at his feet. But Troll's chest feathers were so puffed out that he couldn't see over them. It wasn't until Greta moved the cricket a few feet away that he spotted it. We knew he was interested in it, because he drew himself up until I thought he would fall over backward, nodded his head a few times, and then, suddenly, after three quick hops, pounced on it with both feet.

We expected him to eat it right away, but the cricket wasn't dead yet, and it didn't intend to be. The way Troll had landed, his curved talons didn't crush the insect, but simply arched over it, allowing it to escape between two of his claws. This excited Troll, and he flapped his wings and made a soft gargling noise, while he hopped around the room after the scurrying insect. Finally, Troll made another pounce. This time he pinned his prey, bent over it, and nipped off its head. When he had swallowed this important part, he straightened up. Then he swung his head from side to side, blinked, and let out the most awful squawk I had ever heard come out of that bird's beak. After that, he wolfed down what was left of the poor cricket.

"Gee, that's a good way to exercise his wings," Greta said. "Even if he didn't actually *fly* after the cricket, he sure tried to. Now that it's getting to be spring, we ought to be able to catch a whole lot of insects for him."

I felt speechless from what I had just watched, but I thought I better answer.

"It isn't spring yet," I said. "It's still March."

"It's spring. Our crocuses are up. Anyway, the first day of spring happens in March. Maybe it has already passed."

It did feel like spring. The days were getting longer and a lot more birds were around.

"I'd rather see Troll eat insects than mice," I finally said. "It's not so gross. I'm going to start hunting bugs right away."

"We'll still have to feed him some mice, though," Greta said. "My teacher says he has to have calcium, which he can only get from eating bones and teeth.

McGregor's hair gives him roughage, but it doesn't give him calcium."

Greta's teacher was a big help to us. He had a degree in biology, so science lessons were a lot more interesting at her school than they were at mine. My school had a better library, though. I wondered why the two schools didn't combine. That way, they could offer the best of everything and Greta and I could see more of each other. When we get to junior high, of course, we'll both be in the same school and can be together all the time. That is, if Greta hasn't moved to some other town by then.

Greta's teacher was almost as much help as my school's librarian. Mrs. Freed even ordered a new book for the library at my request. It was about squirrels and it told me that our Nutkin would stay a baby and need care until she was two months old. That's how long a mother red squirrel looks after her pups. The book also gave me a lot of ideas on how to feed Nutkin when the time came to put her on solid food. Her diet was going to be a lot easier than Troll's. We could give her sunflower seeds from my mom's bird feeder, spruce cones from our blue spruce trees, and new leaf buds, right off the oak and maple trees in Greta's backyard.

If Nutkin had been a gray squirrel, instead of a red one, her diet would have been different. A gray squirrel isn't able to open up a spruce cone to get at the seeds inside. It eats acorns, instead. Since acorns don't form on trees until summer, we would have had a terrible time finding any for Nutkin. Only a mother gray squirrel knows where to find acorns in spring. That's because she spent the previous fall burying thousands of them in all kinds of secret places.

I was glad Nutkin was a red squirrel, because I wouldn't have liked for Greta and me to have to hoe up our yards, looking for buried acorns. We would have done it, though. We would have done anything for Nutkin. She was the cutest baby animal I ever saw, and both of us had fallen in love with her.

CHAPTER
SEVEN

As the weather got warmer, we moved the Castle onto a screen porch at the back of Greta's house and we took Troll out in the yard for his flying lesson every day. There was no danger that he would get away from us because his right wing feathers had not grown far enough in yet.

Nutkin was keeping everyone busy. Even Greta's brother, Albert, sometimes gave her a bottle when no one else was home. Greta's dad, of course, had the most to do.

I don't know what we would have done if Mr. Mallard had gotten hired someplace. There didn't seem to be much danger of that happening, though. He didn't even go on interviews anymore. Just sat around the house looking glum.

You would think we had enough to do caring for Troll and Nutkin, but we were soon to become a kind of emergency center for wildlife. After my talk at school, kids began to bring sick and baby animals to us. The next patient to arrive was a chipmunk, which a girl in my class had taken away from her cat. It didn't have any wounds that we could see—it just seemed to be in shock. Greta's mother suggested we put it in a box and leave the box in a dark and quiet place. We did this, but when we looked in on it later, the chipmunk was dead.

I felt really bad. We probably should have done something more than we did. But what? The chipmunk must have been hurt in some way that we couldn't see. And even if we had found the problem, we really didn't know how to treat an injury. Thank goodness, none of the other animals that had come to us had had serious problems—just broken wing feathers or poor judgment about where to land. And Nutkin, of course, was a help-less baby, but otherwise healthy.

We buried the little chipmunk in Greta's backyard and marked the place with a stone. I said a prayer over its grave. I don't know if there is a chipmunk heaven, or for that matter, even an animal heaven, but I sure hope there is. Better still, I'd like all animals to go to our heaven. It would make the place a lot more interesting than I usually picture it.

The next animal that came under our care died too. It was a mole, of all things. It had come up from its underground home to eat some seeds that had spilled out of our neighbor's bird feeder, and McGregor grabbed it. When Mr. Marshall, McGregor's master, handed it to me, it was all wet from being carried around in McGregor's mouth, but it was still alive.

Moles are the strangest creatures. They don't have any real eyes—just a place on their heads where they ought to be. After I dried this one off, I felt that I was touching the softest fur of any animal in the world. I had to hold the mole against my cheek, it was so soft. Then I laid it in a box, which I put in a warm, quiet, dark place before going off to look up *mole* in our encyclopedia. When I came back, the poor thing was dead.

Greta and I dug another grave beside the chipmunk's and held a second burial service two days after the first. It was getting to be depressing, all this death. And I felt like we were to blame, because everyone thought we knew how to take care of animals, and we really didn't. Up until now we had done our best and been lucky. But our patients hadn't needed any medical attention, only good care.

Greta felt bad too. She said that she was going to become a veterinarian when she grew up so that she would know better what to do. I thought maybe I would become one, too, although I'm pretty squeamish about taking shots, myself, and could never stick a needle in a dog or a cat. Greta would be a good vet, though. She's a lot tougher about such things than I am.

Thank goodness the next animal that came to us was another baby. We thought we could probably do something for it. Right away, I got on the phone and called McGregor's vet to see what kind of formula I should mix for a raccoon.

"A raccoon? Well, you've got yourselves a handful there. They get into everything, you know."

"It's too little to get into trouble. It's really young. In fact, it doesn't have any teeth yet."

"All the more reason why you should try to put it back with its mother. Where did you find it?"

"Near the airport. The tree it was living in was bulldozed to make room for that new mall they're building out there. One of the construction workers brought it home for his kid, but the kid's mom wouldn't let him keep it. She was scared of rabies."

"She probably heard about the problem they're having in the East. Well, we're fortunate that rabies hasn't hit here. It's at epidemic stages in the eastern states, and if you had told me that this animal had come from that part of the country, I would have had to report it to the state Board of Health and you would have had to be vaccinated. I just hope rabies doesn't spread to our raccoons out here. They are such interesting animals, I would sure hate to see them all die off."

"All die off? Will all the raccoons in the East die?" I asked. It sounded like a terrible plague.

"Every raccoon that has the disease will die. It's fatal. Of course, when there are no more carriers to pass it on, the epidemic will subside."

What the vet told me made me feel more determined than ever to keep our raccoon alive. Dr. Barnes must have felt the same way, because he was wonderfully helpful. He told us how to mix a formula, and he suggested that we wear gloves, so that the baby wouldn't try to cut its teeth on our fingers. Then he came up with a good suggestion.

"Sometime when it's older, you can bring it in for a rabies vaccination," he said. "I don't know if that awful disease will ever come our way, but I'd like to immunize it, just in case. At least then there will be one raccoon that won't get sick and die."

Rocky Star was adorable. We gave him that name because the dark band across his eyes looked like the kind of sunglasses rock stars wear. His grayish fur was coarse to the touch, but nice and thick. And the white whiskers that grew on his pointy nose told us how relaxed or how awake he was. When he was interested in something, they stood straight out like a cat's. When he was sleepy, they lay flat against his face.

He was like a kitten in other ways too. He made a kind of purring sound when he was happy, and he hissed when he was mad. He also washed his face like a cat, first licking his paws until they were all wet, and then rubbing them all over his cheeks and in back of his ears. His paws were not at all like a cat's, though. They had five long fingers and they looked a lot like a person's hands. They could do just about anything a person's hands do, too, such as hold bottles, play with buttons, even open cage latches.

I took out a book from the library that described how a family in Florida had raised a raccoon and then released it. We got a lot of tips from that book. By looking at the pictures, we were able to see that Rocky Star was about six weeks old. When a raccoon is that age, its mother still licks her baby's belly after every meal to make it urinate. We didn't have to do that, thank goodness. Instead, we massaged his belly with a warm sponge.

We already knew about putting a plastic bottle filled with warm water under Rocky Star's bedding. And there were other things, too, that we knew or learned on our own, such as not leaving a dish of water in his box—he used it as a toilet! Nor did we need a book to tell us that he was a great escape artist. A few days after we got him, we discovered that no box was big enough to stop him from crawling over the side.

I don't know how we would have kept him from running all over the place had Mr. Mallard not made us another wonderful cage, this one built around a little tree in Greta's backyard. It was even better than the Castle he had made for Troll. It was bigger and it had a real roof over it. Like Troll's cage, it was taller than it was wide, so that Rocky Star could run up and down the tree that grew inside it. And partway up, there was a resting

platform with a den at one end. There the baby raccoon could hide or sleep.

It was surprising how Rocky Star took to us. When he was hungry, he crawled up on our laps, stuck his pointy face in ours, and made little begging sounds. We played with him a lot, and we held him a lot, and after a while, we started calling him Rocky, for short. He just seemed like a baby brother to us. I suppose he looked at it another way. He must have thought we were his mothers.

Maybe it was living in that tree that made him feel so at home with us. Rocky loved his tree. Most of the time he stayed in it and made almost no use of his resting platform. He could balance and even fall asleep perched on one of the tree's small branches. He looked just like a ball of fur up there with his striped tail wrapped around his face.

To get him to come down to ground level, all we had to do was place a small tub of water at the base of the tree. He liked to drop pebbles and sticks into this and then fish them out again. Sometimes he climbed all the way in. When he did, he took care to hold his tail high in the air, so that it would stay dry and fluffy.

Having a baby raccoon around is like having a human baby to care for, except that a raccoon cub grows a lot faster. Soon we were feeding Rocky baby food from a jar. After that, we added table scraps and fresh fruits and vegetables to his diet.

It's a good thing we did decide to wear gloves when we first got him. As soon as his teeth came in, he nibbled on everything he could find, just as Dr. Barnes had said he would. He also began using his front paws more. To Rocky, touch was more important than sight. He grabbed everything and he wouldn't let go! To make him turn loose our shirt buttons, or worse, our hair, we had to carry a stone or a nut in our pockets. Sometimes we could persuade him to let go of what he was clutching and take one of these, instead.

But the cutest thing our Rocky Star did was to cover his eyes with his hand-like paws when he was frightened. In this respect, he was like an ostrich that buries its head in the sand. Rocky just didn't like to look trouble in the face, even though he loved to create it.

Our feeding schedules got much easier when Rocky began to eat solid food. He still wanted his bottle, but not every two hours. And the same was true for Nutkin. She was no trouble at all, once she began to eat the new spring leaves that were budding on the trees. Greta was able to climb right out of her bedroom window onto a tall tree that grew alongside her house and collect oak buds for her. We also gave Nutkin peanut butter, which she just loved.

I suppose we were too happy with our three animals to think that anything could possibly go wrong. They were all doing so well. Troll was learning to fly again, Rocky Star was growing more beautiful every day, and

Nutkin looked as if she might be ready for release in another month. That was when a snake entered our Garden of Eden.

Please understand that I have nothing at all against snakes. I am not one of those people who believe snakes are slimy and won't touch them. I have touched a lot of snakes, and I know that their skin is as dry as your fingernail. I'm not afraid they will bite me either, unless they happen to be poisonous. What happened was not the snake's fault at all, but the fault of the boy who brought us the snake.

CHAPTER
EIGHT

Russell Collins is not the kind of boy you would want to know. He tries to trip kids when they least expect it, and then he laughs. Still, when he brought us the blind snake, we thought there must be a good side to Russell that nobody knew about. Before it was all over, though, we realized that Russell hadn't brought us the snake for humanitarian reasons. He was just trying to scare us with it. And when we didn't jump and scream and say, "Take it away!" he must have been mighty disappointed. But I'm getting ahead of my story.

We knew the moment we looked at what he was dangling in front of us that it was a garter snake. Both Greta and I had seen garter snakes before and knew they are harmless. So Greta reached out and took the snake from Russell.

"I don't think it likes being held by the tail like you're doing," she said. "It needs to be supported in two places with two hands, like this."

"Yeah, well, I hope it bites you," Russell said, still trying to scare us.

"It can't bite me, because I have a grip on its neck. It can't turn its head to strike at me."

"Snakes don't have necks," Russell hooted. "Snakes are all neck."

Conversations with Russell never got anyplace, so I thought we'd better end this one.

"We'll just take it inside and fix up a box for it," I said. "Thanks for bringing it to our clinic."

After we shut the door, I asked Greta where she had learned to handle a snake.

"I saw it on television," she answered.

Both Greta and I liked to watch a series on public television called *Nature*, but we each got different things from the programs we saw. She noticed how different kinds of animals were handled and fed. What stuck in my mind was how the animals acted with one another.

"Now what on earth are we going to feed this patient?" I wondered out loud.

"Nothing at all," Greta piped up. "Don't you remember? Snakes hardly ever eat. They can go for months and months without food."

"Well, sooner or later it will have to eat something," I insisted.

"I don't think so. If my guess is right, we won't be keeping this snake long enough for it to work up an appetite," Greta replied.

"What do you mean? We can't turn a blind snake loose."

"That's right, but this snake isn't really blind; it's just getting ready to shed its skin. Remember that program we watched on pythons? Their eyes were cloudy like this just before they peeled out of their old, dead skins."

"Oh, I'd forgotten that," I said. Then I burst out laughing. "You didn't feel like mentioning that little fact to Russell, did you?"

"Heck, no! He never would have given us the snake if he thought it had a chance of living."

Greta and I felt really good about putting one over on such a mean boy—especially since the snake would not have lasted long under his care. If smart Greta hadn't reached right out and relieved him of it, he would have carried it around in his pocket and used it to scare kids. Thanks to her, it was now safe with us and would soon be set free. Meanwhile, it didn't need any special attention from us. I was glad to have an animal that didn't need a bottle every two hours. All we had to do for the snake was keep it quiet until it shed its old skin, and that didn't take long to happen.

The very next day, Gertrude the Garter Snake— that's the name we gave her—began to peel. And I do mean peel! Her skin started to curl backward, starting where her lips would have been if snakes had lips. Then, as her long body wriggled out, her old skin turned wrong-side out, like a pulled-off sock. We watched this for hours. The tail part of Gertrude, which was still covered by the old skin, looked drab and ugly, while the front end, where the new skin was showing, was shiny and beautiful. And just as Greta predicted, Gertrude's cloudy eyes, once they had peeled, were bright and beautiful too.

"This is our best success story yet," Greta said. "Where should we turn her loose?"

"In Red Rock Park, near the pond," I said. This kind of snake likes to live near water.

Together we set off on a two-mile hike to the park, carrying a new-looking Gertrude in a brown paper bag.

Turning her loose made us both feel good. We didn't worry at all about how she would make out. Snakes can crawl into holes and take good care of themselves. With no regrets, we let her go. And go she did. In a flash she disappeared, fluttering into the underbrush like a striped hair ribbon.

"Well, that's the end of that," Greta said.

"Yep," I agreed.

Little did we know that it was only the beginning. Two days later, Russell knocked on Greta's door and asked for his snake back. Since I wasn't there at the time, Greta had to handle the situation by herself. What she told me about their conversation really annoyed me.

"He said it was *his* snake, and he never intended to give it to us, only I had grabbed it away from him."

"Then why did he bring it here?" I asked.

"He said he wanted to show it to us."

"Scare us with it is more like it. Well, it serves him right. He must have been surprised when we didn't scare and you plucked it out of his hands."

We both laughed at the memory of that.

"Anyway, when I told him that we didn't have it, he was furious. You should have seen his face."

"Good! Did you tell him that he was dumb to think the snake was blind?"

"No. He was mad enough. He said that we had no business taking in animals—that it's illegal."

"Illegal? What's illegal about it?"

"I don't know, but he threatened to report us to the state Department of Fish and Game."

"But how could it be illegal?"

"I don't know. According to Russell, the public is definitely not allowed to keep wild animals."

"Well, I don't believe it. We're not doing anything bad to Nutkin or Troll or Rocky Star," I said. "We're helping them stay alive until they can survive on their own. We aren't breaking any laws."

Greta agreed that Russell was probably bluffing.

"Well, my dad's a lawyer, and he can defend us if we get arrested or anything."

Over the next few days we were so busy with our patients that we almost forgot about Russell's threat. Our two baby animals had become expert climbers and were all over the place. And Troll was learning to fly again. Every day, we tied a long cord around one of his legs and flew him in Greta's backyard. To make him flap his wings, we tossed him high in the air. This gave him enough lift to carry him some distance. And every day, he was able to travel farther, before making a clumsy landing. It was fun flying him like a kite, and some of the kids in the neighborhood came to watch us do it.

One afternoon, while we were in the backyard flying Troll, we heard the phone ring.

"Do you have to answer?" I asked. "I'll hold Troll's cord."

"No, my dad's home and he'll want to get it. It might be long distance. It could be a job interview," she said.

Hearing this forced me to ask, "Is he looking for a job out of town?"

"He's looking for a job anywhere that he can find one," Greta said. "There are so many unemployed people around here that we might have to move somewhere else."

While she spoke, Greta was squinting into the sun, trying to follow Troll's flight. When the little owl plopped to the ground, I saw that her eyes were tearing, and I thought she might be trying not to cry. Neither of us said any more about the possibility of her having to move. In fact, we didn't talk at all while we put Troll back into his cage.

Afterward, we fed Rocky and Nutkin. The three of our charges had outdoor pens now, thanks to Greta's dad. This made cleaning them much easier. All we had to do was shut the animals up in their sleeping compartments and then go inside their pens with rakes. Now, while we were scraping up droppings, Greta's dad appeared at the back door.

"Girls, come on in," he said. "I need to talk to you."

My first thought was that he had been hired someplace five hundred miles away. But he looked too upset for that. He would have looked happy if he had just landed a job. Maybe somebody died.

"I just got a call from the state Department of Fish and Game," he began after we had sat down.

At these words, Greta's face went white, and my own began to burn, so I knew it was turning red. We waited for him to say more, but he took his time. Finally, he blurted out, "They have some screwball idea that all wildlife belongs to the state."

"They own it all?" Greta asked with disbelief.

"Seems so," her dad replied, his mouth set in a straight line.

"Well then, we should just send them a bill for all the food we've been buying for *their* animals," she said.

Greta and her dad looked alike when they got mad. They acted the same too. The two of them sat there glowering for a full minute. At last, I decided to break the silence.

"Do they want us to turn over our patients to them?" I asked.

"You've got it," Mr. Mallard answered.

Greta was still speechless, so I asked the next question. I could hardly get the words out, though, because I was so afraid of what the answer might be.

"Will they take good care of them?" I finally managed.

"No. They won't do anything for them." Mr. Mallard's voice was almost shaking with rage.

"What do you mean?" I asked.

"You mean they'll *kill* them?" Greta shouted.

Her dad answered in a low voice, "Probably."

"What?" we both cried out together.

"But why?" Greta asked.

"Because the man I talked to says raccoons and screech owls and red squirrels are such common animals that they aren't worth spending time and money on. He said the department called them 'trash' animals. According to him, if you girls had taken in endangered animals, well, then the department would find money to take care of them."

I'd never heard Mr. Mallard say so much at one time, but then I'd never seen him mad before.

"Don't common animals need help when they're sick or hurt or abandoned?" I asked.

"Seems not."

"Well, if the Fish and Game people don't *want* to

take care of common animals, why can't we?" Greta demanded.

"That's the very question I put to that smug bureaucrat."

"What was his answer?"

"He said you can't keep wild animals because they aren't yours. They belong to the state. And if you girls don't turn in your owl, raccoon, and squirrel immediately, he'll come on our property, and seize them."

This was unbelievable. How could we have gotten into such trouble just because we were caring for some animals that needed our help? It didn't make any sense. Could Mr. Mallard have heard right? Well, maybe my dad could clear up the problem. Legal matters are his business, after all. When I reminded Greta and her dad of this fact, they urged me to go straight home and talk to him.

"We're lucky it's Saturday," Mr. Mallard said. "The Fish and Game probably can't get a search warrant until Monday. That gives us tomorrow to work something out."

I ran all the way home and burst in on my dad, who was getting ready to go golfing.

"I'll stop in the office after our game and check out the state statutes on keeping wildlife," he promised.

I never felt more anxious about anything in my life. I was counting on my dad to come up with a solution, but hours passed, and he didn't come home. Meanwhile, Greta called twice. Finally, I heard his car pull up in the driveway. But when he came in, he didn't say anything. I wondered if he had forgotten his promise to check out the law.

"What did you find out?" I asked.

"Let's sit down and talk about this," he said.

My heart sank at these words. It meant a long discussion before I would hear a definite yes or no.

"Can they take our animals?" I demanded to know.

"Lindsay, calm down," he said. "I'm going to explain the legal side of this."

I made myself be quiet, but I was exploding inside.

"To begin with, you must understand that the state has the law on its side. That's important, because this family obeys the law."

I couldn't believe what I was hearing.

"Not only does the state have jurisdiction over the wild animals that you and Greta are keeping, the federal government, under the Migratory Bird Treaty Act, has something to say about the owl you are caring for."

I had to interrupt.

"But they don't really *want* injured animals," I argued. "The man who called told Mr. Mallard that the state wouldn't bother to take care of them because they're not endangered species. He said they would kill them."

I could hardly get all the words out before I began

to sob. My dad put his hand on my shoulder, but I shoved it away.

"Lindsay, I'm so sorry this has happened to you," he said. "Both you and Greta have been doing a fine thing for those animals. I know how much work you have put into caring for them. But the law is clear on this matter. I wish it were otherwise."

"Well, I'm not going to obey the law," I sputtered. "I don't agree with it. Anyway, Troll and Nutkin and Rocky Star are more important than any law! Besides, who made up such a law? God? No! Just a lot of dumb men who think they have the right to kill animals."

"Now, Lindsay, stop and think a minute. Maybe you don't like the law, but you still must obey it. What if everyone decided to obey only those laws that they agreed with? We'd be in big trouble then."

Now I knew what my mother meant when she said that it's impossible to argue with my dad when he puts on his lawyer's cap. He made me so mad that I began to shout.

"You're not on my side," I yelled. "You don't care how I feel or what happens to our animals. You can have your old law. I'm not going to let anyone take away our animals. They'd have to shoot me first."

With those words I ran out of the house and all the way to Greta's. I never wanted to see my dad again. I would leave home and move in with Greta.

CHAPTER NINE

I didn't tell Greta that I had left home for good. I just said that I planned to spend a few nights with her. We often slept over at each other's house, so my coming over didn't seem strange to her. Anyway, she didn't question me about it. That's the way we are with each other. We don't dig into things that are too personal. Just like Greta doesn't like to talk about her dad's being out of work, I didn't want to tell her about having a fight with mine. I would hate to have her think bad things about him, even though *I* was never going to forgive him.

She probably suspected something was wrong, though, especially after I told her what he had said about obeying the law and giving up on our animals. It was kind of embarrassing for me, because both Greta and her dad had counted on my dad to come up with a solution to our problem.

"I don't see why anyone should have to obey a law that kills innocent animals," Greta said, after I had finished telling her.

Of course, that's exactly how I felt too. But how could two girls possibly stand up to a grown-up who is a special agent of some kind? And how could we stop him from bursting into Greta's house and taking Troll, Nutkin, and Rocky Star away?

"Well, they can't take away your animals if they can't find them, now can they?" her dad piped up.

I was startled to hear him say that. I guess I thought all adults were the same and that he would react like my dad had. That's why I didn't get it that he was actually thinking about helping us. Greta caught on, though.

"You mean we might be able to hide them?" she asked. "Where?"

"I'll give that some thought," he replied with a grin.

That evening we went through the usual feeding and flying routine, but my heart was heavy. When I fed Nutkin, all I could think of was that she might not live long enough to be set free. If we weren't able to find a really good hiding place for her, she might never know what being a wild squirrel was all about. She might never know what it was like to make daring leaps from one tree to the next, to store pinecones for winter, to make a nest out of leaves and grass. Poor Nutkin! She would be cheated out of everything that she was born to do.

That night I dreamt that Rocky Star was about to be

shot. In my dream, I saw him holding his paws over his eyes so that he couldn't see the man who was aiming a gun at him. Greta and I were there, but we couldn't get to Rocky to save him. So Greta tried to scare him into running away by banging on a pan.

When I woke up, I realized that the banging sound in my dream had been real. It was Mr. Mallard hard at work in a tree outside Greta's bedroom window. He was building cages in the very oak tree where we had gathered buds for Nutkin to eat. By now, those leaf buds had opened and grown so big that they almost hid him from view.

"Oh, that's a great place to hide the animals," Greta called to her dad. "We can climb into the tree from my window to get to them."

Her dad went on working without answering. When he started a project, he didn't like to discuss it. I remembered that from the time he built Troll's first cage down in the basement.

All that day Greta and I were excited by the thought of the animals being housed in a tree.

"After all, that's the right place for them," Greta said. "Squirrels and raccoons and owls are supposed to live in trees."

"I just hope that the law enforcement agent, or whoever comes, doesn't happen to look up," I said.

"We'll have to distract him so he won't," Greta said. "If he starts toward the tree, you pretend to faint."

"What if our animals make noises, like squeals or squeaks or chitterings?"

"Then we'll start talking really loud and drown them out."

By late afternoon, the cages were ready. Mr. Mallard had covered them with branches so that, unless you knew exactly where to look, you couldn't see them. He seemed really pleased with his work, but as usual, he didn't say anything. He just grinned when we hugged him and thanked him a thousand times.

It was a little tricky moving our animals into their new quarters. First, we wrapped each one in a towel, so it couldn't see or flap or jump while we carried it. Then we took turns. One or the other of us would climb out of the bedroom window, step onto the roof of the porch below, and then climb onto a branch and straddle it like a horse. The other would then pass an animal to her freed-up hands. After that, it was just a matter of scooting along the branch to the animal's waiting cage.

The cages were not as roomy and nice as the ones in the yard, but in a way, they were better for the animals. Not only were they a more natural home, they gave our patients some privacy. Greta and I had always worried about having so much contact with our wild creatures. It made them too trusting, and this could get them into trouble. After we set them free, they might hop or fly or walk right up to the first person they met, expecting them to be as friendly as us.

By the time Greta's mom called us to come in for dinner, all three animals had inspected their new cages and settled down. At the table, I was surprised to see my favorite kind of lasagna being served in a baking dish just like one of ours at home. When I mentioned this, Greta's mom said that Marie had come over with it and brought some school clothes for me, as well. I guess my folks had just accepted the fact that I had left home for good. It hurt to think they would just let me go like that. I wondered what Marie had told Mrs. Mallard about my fight with my dad.

"Tomorrow morning, Greta and Albert and I will leave here at seven o'clock sharp," Greta's mom said to me. "I have to open the school office half an hour before the first bell, so we always leave early. Someone will pick you up at seven-thirty and drive you to your school, Lindsay."

"I can walk," I said. I didn't want to see either of my parents.

"Well, I've been told that you don't have your schoolbooks here. You left them at home. Of course, you will need them tomorrow, so it's best you go along with this plan," Mrs. Mallard replied.

Her words suddenly reminded me that I hadn't done my homework. I could see that the next days were going to be hard. Our animals were in grave danger, we were breaking the law, and my parents didn't seem to care that I'd moved out. I suddenly felt so terrible that a big lump formed in my throat, and I couldn't swallow the lasagna. I held my glass of milk up to my mouth and pretended to drink, so that no one would notice my eyes were filling with tears. Luckily, I was saved when Greta's mom mentioned that there was going to be a film about owls on TV.

"I think it's about to start. Why don't you girls take your plates into the living room and watch it?"

I was sure glad to leave the table before I made a fool of myself. But the program wasn't about owls, after all. It was about wildebeests in Africa. I don't know why Mrs. Mallard thought it was going to be about owls. It was interesting, of course, and we watched it to the end. Then we got Troll out of his cage and gave him a practice flight in the dusky light.

"I wonder why we never flew him at night before," Greta said. "That's when owls actually come out."

"Besides that, it's safer to fly him when your neighbors can't see us doing it," I added.

Troll did just fine in the low light. His eyes were made for the dark. Ours weren't, of course, and soon we had trouble seeing him. So we put him back into his cage along with a fat mouse we had caught. Before passing Troll to Greta on the branch, I pressed him to my cheek and said good-night to him.

"Oh, Troll, I love you," I said. "We promise we

won't betray you, no matter what. I think I'd rather die first."

The next morning I was in for the shock of my life. Right after Greta, her mom, and Albert had left for her school, the doorbell rang. I was waiting in the living room for someone to pick me up and take me to my school, so I answered it. But instead of my mom or dad, a strange man in a brown uniform was standing there.

"Is this the Mallard residence?" he asked.

"Who is it?" Mr. Mallard called from the kitchen.

"A conservation officer from the state Department of Fish and Game. I have an order here to pick up some animals," he called back.

Now I was on my own. I was so scared that I thought my legs would give way. And when I opened my mouth to speak, no words came out. Fortunately, Greta's dad came up behind me.

"Is this your daughter?" the man asked him.

"No," he answered.

I could tell by the look on the conservation officer's face that he thought Mr. Mallard was lying.

"This order says that your daughter, here, is harboring wild animals in your home." Then he looked straight at me. "Are you aware that what you are doing is illegal?"

"This is not my daughter, I told you. My daughter is in school," Mr. Mallard said.

"What's your name, young lady?" the man asked.

I was still speechless. I guess it didn't matter, though, because he went right on talking to me, as if I were Greta.

"This order says that you have at least two mammals and a bird in your possession, namely, *Tamiasciurus hudsonicus, Procyon lotor,* and *Otus asio.* It further says that you have been informed by telephone conversation that holding these animals in captivity violates a state statute, which prohibits unlicensed individuals from harboring wildlife. You were further informed that keeping a migratory bird is prohibited by federal law. You were also ordered to deliver these animals to our headquarters on Saturday, but did not appear. I am now here to confiscate them."

Even if I could have gotten some words out, I was saved from having to do so by Mr. Mallard, who really sounded angry.

"First of all, I told you that this little girl is not my daughter," he said. "In the second place, I don't know what language you speak, sounds like Greek or Latin to me. This girl and I aren't versed in those tongues, so you'd better come back with a translator."

Mr. Mallard was about to close the door when the officer elbowed his way right into the house, saying, "I have a warrant here to search your premises. Let me pass, please."

The next few minutes were torture. Greta's dad and

I trailed after him, as he looked in every room, every closet, every cupboard. He even rattled around in the basement. Then he asked how to get into the attic. Mr. Mallard got a ladder and let him climb up through a trapdoor. After that, he went into the backyard and looked at the empty cages where we had kept Troll, Nutkin, and Rocky Star before we hid them in the tree. Next, he looked in the garage. There he saw some traps we had set to catch mice for Troll. I wondered what he would make of that. Then twice he walked around the house, passing right under the tree where our animals were caged. Both times I held my breath until I thought I would pass out. Luckily, the animals didn't make a sound, and the officer never thought to look up. Finally, all three of us ended up in the front yard. There he muttered something about how we must have given the animals to somebody else to hold.

"I can see recent signs that animals have been fed around here, and I now order you to tell me where they are."

He directed this command at me, and when I didn't answer, he repeated it.

"I order you to tell me what you have done with the wild animals you have been holding here."

I could feel my legs shaking and was trying hard to think of what to say when, suddenly, I heard someone shout, "Don't answer him, Lindsay."

The voice was my father's. He had just arrived to

drive me to school and was coming up the walk.

"Who are you?" the agent asked him.

"I am this girl's father. I am also an attorney," he answered. "And who are *you*?"

"I am a conservation officer for the state Department of Fish and Game," the man shot back.

"May I suggest to you that it is unbecoming for a state officer to behave in an intimidating manner toward a child? Come, Lindsay, get into the car, or you'll be late for school."

Never, ever, in my whole life was I so glad to see anybody. My dad gave me a big hug, and I just burst into tears. I wasn't sad. They were tears of relief. I had been so scared that the officer would find our animals, and it felt so good to be with my dad again. Suddenly, things seemed like they might work out.

As we drove to school, my dad fished a handkerchief out of his pocket and handed it to me.

"We hope you will come home now, Lindsay," he said. "We sure miss you. The place doesn't seem the same without our girl. How about it?"

It was hard for me to speak, because I was still crying a little.

"I want to," I managed to say, "but I can't turn over the animals to that man. He'd kill them. I can't obey the law, no matter what. I'll go to jail first."

We were at school by then, and my dad parked the car and turned to me.

"Wipe your eyes and look at me, Lindsay. I have something to say to you."

I did as he said.

"I'm really proud of you, my girl. You are very young to take a stand against the law as a matter of conscience, but I see that that is what you are doing. The law is not going to excuse you for it, however. People who break laws, even bad laws, must pay the penalty. Yet, sometimes, people of conscience are willing to stand up for what they believe is right, and willing to take the punishment for doing so. As a result, they call attention to laws that need to be changed. Still, they have to pay a price for their belief. Do you understand that?"

"I think so."

"Here's an example. More than twenty years before you were born, African-American people in the South refused to obey unjust laws that said they could not sit in the front of a bus or eat in an all-white restaurant. Well, they defied those laws and sat where they pleased. And hundreds of them were hauled off and put into jails for breaking the law. Well, pretty soon the jails were full, and the entire country had heard about what was going on. Almost everybody sided with the African-American cause and demanded that the unjust laws be changed. So, in the end, the law was changed. That kind of lawbreaking is called civil disobedience."

"Is that what Greta and I are doing?"

"I think so. If I have heard you right, you said that

you would be willing to go to jail to protect your animals. That's very brave of you, and I can't ask you to act against your conscience. Now are you ready to come home again?"

At that moment, I loved my dad so much that I couldn't say anything. I just threw my arms around him and kissed him. Then I got out of the car and went into the school quickly. I needed time to wash my face before going to class.

CHAPTER
TEN

Even though I had moved back home, most of my free time was spent at Greta's, helping with the animals. It was exciting taking care of them now that we had to keep their whereabouts a secret. One of us always looked to see if the coast was clear before the other hauled food or water into the tree. Even so, the man next door noticed us.

"I see your dad built you a tree house," he said one day. "I had one of those as a kid. Spent a lot of time in it, too, just like you girls. Only in my day, it was the boys who liked to climb trees. Girls knew how to be ladies. I guess times have changed, though, what with women's lib and all."

Greta rolled her eyes at this remark, but we let it pass. What we were up to was much too serious to risk getting into an argument over a sexist remark. We just left it that we were playing house in a tree.

Troll's nightly practice sessions were paying off. Now when we tossed him, he stayed airborne and circled, instead of just fluttering to the ground.

"It's time to liberate him," Greta announced one day.

I hated to say good-bye to such a nice bird, but I couldn't argue with the fact that his wing feathers had grown back. Still, I had reservations.

"How do we know he can catch food for himself? He hasn't had to hunt during the whole time he's been here."

"He knows where to look for mice. Don't forget, he wasn't exactly a baby when we got him."

I could see that Greta was dead set on freeing the owl. On the other hand, she could see that I wasn't at all keen on the idea.

"Come on," she said. "We can't keep him in a cage forever, just because we like him. He'll do okay."

I thought about this for a while, trying to come around to her way of thinking. What really bothered me was that, once we set him free, we would never know if he made it or not.

"That's always going to be the case," Greta said.

She was right, of course. Besides, he'd sure be better off on his own than in the hands of the Fish and Game officer. And we expected another visit from him at any time. Then I thought of still another reason to let him go.

"Once Troll is free," I said, "we'll only be guilty of breaking one, not two laws. The Migratory Bird Treaty Act doesn't apply to Nutkin and Rocky Star."

Greta looked at me kind of funny.

"Are you getting cold feet about breaking the law?" she asked in an accusing tone of voice.

"No, not at all," I was quick to answer.

The fact was, though, that what we were doing was on my mind a lot. I had to wonder what kind of punishment we'd get, if we were caught and convicted. That night I asked my dad about it.

"Actually, because you girls are under age, it's your parents who must take responsibility for your actions. I expect I will have to argue your case before a judge," he said.

"Will you win?"

"I don't know."

"Will *you* have to go to jail?"

"Let's not look down the road too far," he said. "I said I would stand behind you on this, and I'll do what I can."

Suddenly, I thought of Mr. Mallard.

"What about Greta's dad? Will he be held responsible?"

"Yes, I'm afraid he will. He is well aware of what his daughter is doing."

I had no choice but to explain all this to Greta.

"It doesn't matter," she said. "My dad wouldn't care

if they did put him in jail. He's that mad about all of this."

But I could see that Greta was troubled by what I had told her, and I tried to reassure her.

"It'll all be over when Nutkin and Rocky Star are old enough to be released," I said. "Meanwhile, we can liberate Troll whenever you say. Probably the best time is at night, don't you think?"

Greta agreed, and the very next night Mr. Mallard drove us to the spot where he and Greta had picked up the owl seven months before.

Troll seemed excited when Greta removed the long cord we always tied to one of his legs during practice flights. Now, perched on her glove, he was free to take off. But he didn't. Instead, he made chittering noises and began turning his head from front to back, and then from back to front, as if he were taking his bearings.

"Fly, Troll, if you are ready," Greta said over and over.

But Troll wasn't in a hurry.

"Stay, Troll, if you aren't," I began chanting.

It was like picking petals off a flower to "she loves me, she loves me not," and waiting to see which way it would come out. Then, suddenly, Troll spread his wing feathers wide apart and swooped off, just as Greta said, "Fly, Troll, if you are ready," for about the twentieth time.

We couldn't hear his wings flap because owls fly

silently. And we couldn't see where he went. It was too dark. But about five minutes later, we heard his laughing sound, a kind of a garble of noise, running down the scale.

"He's saying good-bye and thank you to you girls," Mr. Mallard said.

"Oh, he is, he is," Greta said, clapping her hands. "Oh, I'm so happy he's free. Aren't you glad, Lindsay?"

I, definitely, was happy. All our hard work and worry had been worth it for those last minutes with him. I knew I would remember this night all my life.

We didn't release Troll a minute too soon. The next day the Fish and Game officer paid a surprise visit to the Mallards. I wasn't there, but Greta told me that he searched the place from top to bottom and was mad when he didn't find anything.

"Luckily, I had just raked up Troll's castings," Greta said. "Otherwise, he might have found them and looked up into the tree."

"Did he ask you what you had done with the animals? What did you say? Were you scared? Did he threaten to arrest you?"

"It didn't make any difference what he asked me. My dad told me to 'take the Fifth'—in other words, to say nothing."

"I wish I had been there," I said.

Then I wondered—had those words actually come out of my mouth? Only a short time back, I had been scared witless by the state officer. Now I was ready to meet him head on!

This was all so confusing that I put it out of my mind. In another two weeks, Nutkin would be ready for release. After that, if we got caught, we would only have the one charge against us of keeping Rocky Star. Meanwhile, we were saving lives. And nothing in the world could be more important than that!

I guess my schoolwork suffered as a result of what was going on. At least, my teacher, Mrs. Carlyle, accused me of being distracted and asked me to stay after school for a talk.

"Is something troubling you?" she asked.

"No, nothing," I answered.

"Do you have family problems?"

"Oh, no! Everything is fine at home."

"How about friends? I never see you hang around with any of the girls in your class."

"My best friend goes to Horace Mann," I answered. "I see her nearly every day."

"Oh, well, that explains it. But you are such a lovely girl, I should think you would have lots of friends."

I was so relieved to end that interview that I ran all the way home and did some homework before going to Greta's.

By now we were wearing gloves while handling *both* the animals. Rocky was gripping our wrists really hard and Nutkin's teeth had come in. That little squirrel didn't know the difference between a walnut and the end of a finger. She was taking solid food now. Often, when we had her out of her cage to feed her, she would scramble out of our hands, run up our arms, and onto our heads. Once, she escaped and made it all the way to the top of the tree. Greta had to climb way up among the weakest branches to retrieve her. Then, just as she grabbed Nutkin with one hand, the branch she was standing on broke, and she had to quickly wrap her free arm and one leg around the tree trunk. There she dangled, trying to feel for a foothold, until I could climb up to her, grab one of her feet, and place it on a good solid branch. During all of that, she never let go of Nutkin. You can depend on Greta when it comes to animals.

It was clear that what Nutkin needed was space to practice climbing. The sad thing was that we had just the place for that in her old cage, now sitting empty in the yard. But we didn't dare put her back there, not even for a few minutes. We couldn't take a chance that the neighbors would see her, in case the Fish and Game officer should think to question them. So instead, we took her into the house by way of Greta's bedroom window and let her climb about on the furniture. Even those sessions couldn't last long, though. We never knew when the officer might return.

One day Mrs. Freed stopped me in the hall at school to say she had ordered a magazine she thought would interest me. She was right about that. It was called *Wildlife Rehabilitation Today,* and it contained all kinds of useful advice about caring for wild animals. Some of the articles confirmed that what Greta and I had been doing for animals had been correct. Others, however, made me wonder how we had managed to bungle through.

For example, there was a section on euthanasia, which means putting a badly injured animal out of its misery by killing it. I had never given a moment's thought to such a thing. What if Nutkin or Rocky Star or Troll had come to us with terrible injuries? We couldn't have let them suffer and suffer. But neither Greta nor I would have known how to kill them in a painless way. Besides, it would have been just awful to have to do something like that.

Then there was a long article about orphaned animals that must be raised on a bottle. If possible, you should keep them in a cage with others of their kind, so they will learn what type of animal they are. Otherwise, they might never find out, and after they are released, they won't know how to attract a mate. Well, we couldn't have caged our squirrel or our owl or our raccoon with others of their kind because we only had one of each. The article was written for people who take in lots and lots of animals, and that's what mystified me. Who is allowed to keep wild animals, if all wild animals are owned by the states?

I showed the magazine to Greta, and she and I

searched through it for an answer to that question.

"Look at this," she said at last, pointing to a long list of rehabilitation centers on a back page. "These places are legal, I guess. Otherwise, they wouldn't be making their addresses public. It says here that they are licensed."

It seemed strange to us that some people should be allowed to take care of sick and injured animals, while others, namely us, are persecuted for doing so.

"How do you suppose they got to be licensed?" I wondered out loud.

"I don't know, but let's find out." Greta sounded really excited. "Maybe we can become legal!"

"I'll ask Mrs. Freed to help. She knows how to get just about any book or magazine there is."

That meant I would have to let her in on our secret. Luckily for us, when I told her about how the state officer was trying to take away our animals, she was completely sympathetic. She didn't even ask where we had hidden them.

Two days later, she handed me a book called *The Wildlife Rehabilitator's Study Guide,* and I plunged right into the first chapter. What I read surprised me. Most states (including ours) *do* license certain people to care for injured and orphaned wildlife, but first a person has to take a written exam to show how much she knows about housing, feeding, and caring for different kinds of animals. This was great news. Between the two of us, I felt sure that Greta and I could pass that test.

At first glance the second requirement seemed like a shoo-in. All we needed was proof that we had no criminal record.

Whoa! Wait a minute! What if Rocky Star and Nutkin were found? Wouldn't that make us lawbreakers? Well, I'd worry about that problem when, and if, we got caught.

It was the third requirement that put real doubt in my mind. A state wildlife official would have to visit and evaluate our property and interview us in person.

Help! If that state interviewer turned out to be the same man who was trying to take away our animals, we would never pass.

But it was the fourth and last requirement that dashed any hope of our going straight. Just to apply for a license, we had to be sixteen years old or more.

So much for being legal!

When I reported all of this to Greta, she seemed really depressed.

"Don't worry," I consoled her. "We'll be sixteen someday. Until then, we'll just go on being outlaws."

She didn't answer at first. And, when she did speak, her voice was so low I almost couldn't hear her.

"It's not just the animals," she murmured.

"What else then?" I asked.

There was a long pause. Finally she blurted out, "We're moving. My dad's found a job in Bridgeville."

I sat right down on the floor of her living room and rested my forehead on my knees. It felt like someone had socked me in the stomach. I couldn't utter a word. I just rocked back and forth.

"We'll leave as soon as school is over."

I didn't look up at Greta. Her voice was quavering, and I was afraid we both might start crying. I didn't say anything, either. What was there to say except that being a kid is the pits? Kids are powerless and adults make decisions that tear apart our friendships. Adults try to seize our animals and won't let us take a test we could pass. Being a kid is the pits.

CHAPTER
ELEVEN

It was awful seeing a FOR SALE sign on Greta's house. I had spent so much time there that the place felt like a second home to me. The yard, the basement, Greta's bedroom, the dining room, the kitchen, the living room, the oak tree, the garage, the porch roof—all these places reminded me of the good times we had had together. And now it was all coming to an end.

"It's a good thing Greta's father found a job," my mom said. "Greta's grandmother can use the money from the house sale to go into a nursing home."

I don't think my mom meant to hurt me with that remark, but she did. Adults see the whole world in terms of what is good for other adults. Greta's grandmother didn't love that house. She just owned it.

Greta felt terrible too. We had to make some fast decisions about the animals. Nutkin would be set free in Greta's yard, where we could set out walnuts and birdseed and spruce cones for her to find and eat. That way, she could come and go as she pleased until she was ready to seek her fortune elsewhere.

It was hard just opening the cage door and letting her loose. I was scared that she would run into a neighbor's yard and get caught by a dog or a cat. To prevent this, we filled her cage with goodies and left the door wide open, hoping to lure her back. Sure enough, she returned at night to sleep and eat.

"That goes to show that even a squirrel can learn to like its prison," Greta's dad said when we told him.

I slept over at the Mallards' a lot during those last weeks Greta and I had together. Often in the morning, we heard Nutkin jump from the oak tree and scamper across the roof of the house. It cheered me up to think of her being free at last and able to run where she pleased. I was thankful that Roy had brought her to us, instead of standing by when his father was about to kill her. She was so full of life and energy. Being a squirrel must have seemed like a lot of fun for her.

She knew us too. When we put out walnuts in Greta's backyard, she hopped right over and began to eat them in front of us. When Greta's dad put out walnuts, though, she didn't dare come close.

"I don't think she'll be overly trusting of the new people who move in here," he said. "She knows who her friends are, that's for sure."

There was still the problem of Rocky Star. Even if he were old enough to be set free, once liberated, he would surely get himself into trouble. He was just too clever with his front paws. Early on, he had figured out how to unlatch his cage door, making it necessary for us to tie a rope around it. Now he needed toys to keep his hand-like paws busy. He loved to play with shells and stones and nuts, rolling them around in his fists until they were polished. Sometimes he dropped them into his water dish, just so he could fish them out again.

"It's only a matter of time before he learns how to untie that rope," Mr. Mallard said. "He needs more exercise than he can get in the tree cage. Maybe you should give him some time in the yard cage."

But we were afraid he would be seen by a nosy neighbor and we would be reported to the state Fish and Game. So, instead, we brought him into the house every afternoon and let him run around and attack things. He loved to pounce on the broom when Greta's mom swept the floor. Once, he tried to climb the drapes and brought the whole works down, rod and all.

"That's all right," Greta's mom said. "I have to pack those things, anyway."

Although he was still on a bottle, we now added fresh fruit, canned dog food, and baby food to his diet. These were items that my mom donated to the cause. After eating, he would curl up into a fuzzy ball and nap on Greta's or my lap. And just before dropping off to sleep, he would purr like a kitten.

Greta and I worried a lot about Rocky's future. Normally, a baby raccoon stays with its mother until it's a year old. It learns many things from her, things we couldn't possibly teach Rocky Star. An article in *Wildlife Rehabilitation Today* said that young raccoons should be caged with one or two others of their kind, and later, they all should be released together. That way they learn from one another. Poor Rocky! He didn't have any buddies to hang out with.

"Well, I'll just have to take him with me to Bridgeville, I guess," Greta said.

It really hurt to think that I would soon lose both Greta and Rocky Star. My life was certainly going to be dull after they left. At least Greta would have the excitement of going to a new place. And she would still have Rocky Star to love. Maybe she would forget all about our friendship. Probably someone else would become her best friend and help her take care of Rocky.

"You mustn't be so depressed," my mom told me. "You'll see Greta. She's only going to live fifty miles from here, and you can invite her for a weekend, from time to time."

A weekend! We had been inseparable since we were six years old. My mom really didn't understand.

"I've been meaning to bring this up," she went on. "Your teacher called to say that you have not been paying attention in class. You know, you really must get hold of yourself, Lindsay. You must think of your future. Greta is important to you now, but that will change. What is happening is the best thing for Greta's future. If her father hadn't landed that job, she probably would never go to college. And she is such a bright girl. Didn't you say she wants to become a veterinarian? You should be glad for her."

I had a hard time listening to all of this. Maybe I *was* being selfish by not thinking about Greta's future. To tell the truth, though, I could hardly imagine some far distant time when Greta and I would go to college, much less feel anything about it. It certainly didn't matter to me as much as what was going on in the here and now.

My mom continued, "You'll be going to junior high soon. You'll make a lot of new friends there."

This was one of those one-way conversations that parents have with their kids, so I wasn't expected to say anything. Still, my mind was answering her every statement.

New friends? What was the point of making new friends? Friends go away and leave you.

"Well, I'm awfully glad we've had this little talk," Mom said at last. "I hope we feel much better now."

I guess this was my week for having talks, because the very next day, Mrs. Carlyle asked me to stay after school for a chat. She didn't beat around the bush, but got right to the heart of what she wanted to talk about.

"Your mother tells me that your best friend is moving to another town," she said. "That must make you feel pretty sad."

"Well, it's all for the best. Her dad needs the work so she can go to college someday."

Mrs. Carlyle made a face. "Is that what you really think?"

I could see that she agreed with me that what happens years and years down the line can't feel as important as what is happening now.

"Why don't you tell me about your friendship," she suggested. "What did you two girls like to do together?"

That's when I told her about all the animals we had saved, about the snapping turtles, the owl, the grebe, the blind snake, the red squirrel, and the raccoon. I even told her how Greta and I had tried to save caterpillars when we were only six years old. And when I finished talking, she said, "I think you have a right to feel sad. You girls had so many wonderful experiences together. Hearing all of this, I'm almost envious. Not many people have enjoyed such wonderful adventures with a good friend like Greta."

That's when I just broke down and cried. And Mrs. Carlyle let me go on crying for a long time, without telling me to stop or anything.

"I'm sure your friendship will withstand distance,"

she said at last. "Maybe you won't see each other on a daily basis anymore, but I believe with all my heart that your friendship will last a lifetime."

I think I felt a little better after that.

The following day our librarian handed me the latest issue of *Wildlife Rehabilitation Today* and I spotted something at the back of the magazine that interested me. A new name and address had been added to the list of wildlife rehabilitation centers, and this one was in Bridgeville, of all places. When I showed it to Greta, she got excited.

"Maybe if I get to know the people who run the place, they'll let me help out there," she said.

"Then you could ask them to put Rocky Star in a cage with some other raccoons, so that he can learn whatever it is that he needs to know," I quickly added.

"Yes, but we better inspect the place carefully and meet the people before we trust them with Rocky," Greta said.

As luck would have it, Greta's parents were driving to Bridgeville on the weekend to look for a house to rent, and they agreed to take us along and drop us at the rehabilitation center. But first, we had to wrangle an invitation to visit the place. Greta, being the better talker, got on the phone and explained to the husband and wife who ran the place that we had raised and released some wild animals. She didn't let on that we were kids, though, and

I almost smothered myself in a pillow, trying to keep from laughing out loud at the language she used.

"We are relocating, due to a job transfer, and will have to find temporary accommodations for a juvenile raccoon," she said.

It worked. They said they would be glad to meet us that Saturday.

You wouldn't believe the looks on their faces when they answered their front door and saw us. After their first shock, however, they were really nice about Greta's fooling them, especially when we told them about all the animals we had saved and the trouble that we were having with the state Fish and Game.

"I thought at first that you were selling Girl Scout cookies," Ellen, the woman, said with a laugh.

Joe, her husband, took us around to the back, where pen after pen was set up with every kind of animal inside. They even had a fox with a splint on his leg.

"This little guy was dragging around a leghold trap when some kind soul found him and brought him here," Joe said. "He needed a lot of medical attention, but he'll be all right soon, and then we'll let him go."

"Are you a veterinarian?" Greta asked.

"No," he said. "The state won't grant a rehabilitator's license to a veterinarian."

"Why not?" Greta asked.

"Beats me."

"Who put his leg in a splint?" she asked.

"Oh, I had to take this one to a vet and foot the bill. Wild animals, you know, don't have money to pay for their keep."

"But does the state give you money, I mean, being as you have a license and all?" I asked.

"As its name suggests, the state Department of Fish and Game is funded almost entirely by license fees collected from hunters, fishermen, and trappers. Those groups don't want their money wasted on foxes with broken legs."

"So, how do you buy food and medicine for all these animals?" Greta asked.

"Strictly from donations."

"If we bring Rocky Star here, my dad will give you a donation, I'm sure," I said to Joe.

Greta looked embarrassed, and I realized that she felt she should be volunteering some money too.

"Can I help out here?" she asked. "I could work for Rocky's board. I'm used to cleaning out cages and feeding baby animals."

"I'd be proud to have a helper like you," Joe said.

Greta clapped her hands for joy. Then she saw my face.

"Can Lindsay help too? She'll be visiting me a lot on weekends."

"Absolutely," Joe answered.

"We don't need to be licensed?" I asked.

"No, Ellen and I are licensed. As long as we supervise our volunteers, they don't need licenses."

The ride back to Oakdale was a lot happier than the ride to Bridgeville had been. It wasn't going to be all over between Greta and me, after all. I was certainly going to visit her on weekends whenever I could. And she and I would go on working with animals at the rehabilitation center. Just as importantly, we had found a place where Rocky Star could learn how to be a smart raccoon.

Greta's parents seemed happy too. They talked about the house they had found and said they were sure we would like it. What was going to be Greta's bedroom window looked over a ravine where there were lots of birds and animals. During the ride home, Greta spotted three hawks and I passed around cookies that Marie had baked for me to take along. All was beginning to seem right with the world again. That is, until we pulled up in front of Greta's house. There, parked across the street, was the Fish and Game officer's van.

My heart just about stopped.

"Now what is that guy doing here? Doesn't he have anything better to do than hound little girls?" Mr. Mallard sounded really mad, as he piled out of the car and stalked over to the van.

Greta and I stayed in the car and squeezed each other's hands, while we tried to hear what was being said. Although we could only catch some phrases, we picked up enough so we could fill in the blanks.

"You could have told the girls that there are places where they could take their animals, places where people are *licensed* to care for them."

"That's not my job . . ."

"Do your superiors know you behave like this?" (We couldn't hear the rest of this.)

More mumbling.

Then the officer came on really strong.

"The department is in the business of managing populations and habitats. We aren't funded to act on behalf of every bleeding heart that wants to save trash animals."

"You are unreal," Mr. Mallard shouted. "And do you know what else? You are so dense that you believe *animals* are unreal. Well, these little girls just happen to have some understanding of what's really real and what's not. They don't need a fancy education and a uniform to know that the animals they have cared for so lovingly have value in their own right. Now get out of here."

When we heard the ignition start up, Greta and I breathed a long sigh of relief. But we were still worried that Rocky might be in the van that was pulling away. We waited until it turned the corner; then we leapt from the car, ran upstairs, stepped out of the window, and climbed the tree. And when we peered into his cage, there was Rocky, curled up like a fuzz ball, fast asleep.

We were so happy that we almost fell out of the tree hugging each other. Greta woke up the baby raccoon, and together we gently lowered him onto the porch roof and through the bedroom window.

"Rocky, you're going to a place where you'll meet a lot of raccoons, just like yourself," Greta said. "And Lindsay and I will visit you often and make sure that you have plenty of toys and are happy. Then someday, we'll find a good place for you to live and release you there."

"Maybe that ravine in back of your new house?" I suggested.

"Maybe!"

Then Greta and I hugged each other again. Everything was going to be all right.